"Are you as easily shocked as your mother?"

"Maybe by your standards I am."

Rachel glared at Claudio disapprovingly, resisting the urge to fold her arms across her chest. That would definitely make her look uptight and puritanical, and what she wanted was to look as cool and in command of the situation as he was.

"I wonder, are all English women puritanical?"

"Why don't you go over to England and find out for yourself?"

Stephanie Howard was born and brought up in Dundee, Scotland, and educated at the London School of Economics. For ten years she worked as a journalist in London on a variety of women's magazines, among them *Woman's Own*, and was latterly editor of the now defunct *Honey*. She has spent many years living and working abroad—in Italy, Malaysia, the Philippines and in the Middle East.

Books by Stephanie Howard

HARLEQUIN ROMANCE
3373—THE BEST FOR LAST

Dangerous
Pretence
Stephanie Howard

Harlequin Books

TORONTO • NEW YORK • LONDON
AMSTERDAM • PARIS • SYDNEY • HAMBURG
STOCKHOLM • ATHENS • TOKYO • MILAN
MADRID • WARSAW • BUDAPEST • AUCKLAND

ISBN 0-373-17268-0

DANGEROUS PRETENCE

First North American Publication 1996.

CHAPTER ONE

RACHEL pushed open the shutters and stepped out on to the sunlit balcony, breathing in the sweet green scents of Tuscany. What perfect peace, she thought to herself contentedly as she gazed out over the lush, hilly countryside at the olive groves and vineyards and the dark green cypresses, like pointing fingers against the sapphire of the sky. And she smiled as down below her in the villa garden a cricket chirped lazily in the afternoon heat. So there was someone else besides herself who wasn't having a siesta!

She clasped the iron railings and leaned against them, shaking back the mass of bright red curls from her shoulders and remembered what her friend Abigail had told her two days ago as she'd waved her off at Heathrow Airport.

'It's been a painful, difficult time for you, but the change will do you good. You'll see, in no time you'll have forgotten all the traumas.'

Rachel smiled now. It seemed that Abigail had been right. Here at her mother's beautiful villa at San Cappano, just outside Florence, she could already feel the sense of shock and confusion that had turned her inside out over the past couple of weeks thankfully start to recede a little. She was starting to breathe easier again. All the traumas were over.

5

A picture of Mark—the cause of all her turmoil—flitted across her brain for a moment. Now that he'd gone from her life she knew she would miss him. For they'd known each other a long time and they'd had good times together. And she was sorry it had had to end the way it had, for the last thing she'd ever wanted to do was to hurt him.

She sighed now. The trouble was he'd given her no choice. She was fond of Mark, but there was no way she would ever consider marrying him.

Then she shook herself. Stop brooding, she told herself sharply. Wasn't that why she was here? To forget what had happened. For at the end of two tense and painful weeks—for Mark had refused to accept her 'no' immediately—suddenly she'd been struck by a divine inspiration. Surely this was the perfect moment to take up her mother's long-standing invitation to visit her and her husband Dino in Tuscany? After all, it was the summer break and Rachel had nothing else planned.

A single phone call had been all it took.

'We'd love to see you!' her mother had told her. And that very same day Rachel had gone to her local travel agents and booked herself a seat on the first available flight.

She leaned lightly against the balcony railings now and took a deep, relaxing breath. Mind you, she'd had a few surprises since her arrival—like the sudden, abrupt departure yesterday morning of her mother and Dino to visit friends in Capri. But, though she was on her own now, she had no regrets about coming.

Here in this beautiful, peaceful place she would soon be able to stitch her tattered nerves back together.

It was at that very moment that the peace was shattered.

Suddenly, a huge black and silver motorbike was roaring up the villa driveway, scattering gravel in all directions, to come to a halt directly below Rachel's balcony. Rachel peered down at the broad-shouldered, leather-jacketed figure who sat astride it. Did he have to make quite so much din? she wondered crossly.

She leaned over the balcony and called down, 'Can I help you?' Who was he? she was wondering. She wasn't expecting any visitors!

But the leather-jacketed stranger appeared not to hear her. Without a glance in her direction he was dismounting from the bike and striding across the gravel towards the front door. An instant later the doorbell was shrilling into life.

Wretched man! Rachel turned on her heel irritably and darted back into the bedroom behind her as the shrilling continued unabated downstairs. He must have put his finger on the bell and left it there!

She hurried across the room. Damned impertinence! For all he knew, she might have been having a siesta! As soon as she got downstairs, she'd give him a piece of her mind!

But out on the landing she stopped dead in her tracks. The shrilling had stopped, but what was going on? The front door had been flung open and her unwanted visitor was standing right in the middle of the hall!

'*Dino!*' he was thundering. '*Dov'e il diavolo sei?*'

Rachel leaned over the banisters, her cheeks pink with indignation. 'What's going on? Who do you think you are, barging in here without an invitation?'

'And who the devil are you?'

Instead of offering some explanation, the stranger swung round arrogantly to face her, tilting back his head of glossy, jet-black hair. And as she looked into his face Rachel recognised him instantly.

She had seen this face once before in a photograph. A face so striking it was unforgettable. This man who stood scowling at her was Claudio del'Angelo, her mother's husband's odious nephew.

And there could be only one reason why he was here, it occurred to her. To make trouble for his uncle Dino. According to her mother, that was one of his favourite pastimes. Well, he was in for a disappointment because Dino wasn't here!

But Rachel kept that piece of information to herself for the moment. She began to descend the stairs as he continued to scowl at her. 'I'm Rachel Bennet,' she told him, answering his question. 'Dino's wife's daughter,' she added in case the name meant nothing.

'Emily's daughter?' Claudio raised one dark eyebrow. 'So, you're Emily's schoolteacher daughter, are you? Now that's a surprise. Particularly in the circumstances.'

'What circumstances?'

Rachel had now reached the second stair from the bottom and that was as far as she was prepared to descend, she had decided. If she descended any further, this tall, dark man before her would end up towering over her like some Titan. And, even on this level, he was already quite dominant enough!

It was that extraordinary face of his that gave him his air of dominance and Rachel found herself studying it in silence for a moment, reflecting that he was even more striking than his photograph—something that, quite frankly, she would not have believed possible.

It was a face that spoke of passion and pride and power, with its strong, straight nose, wide, sensual mouth and eyes as deep and black as midnight. Every perfectly sculpted, deeply tanned line of it proclaimed a character destined to be master, not servant. And those eyes, with their arrogant gaze, were the eyes of an emperor.

He wore his glossy black hair pushed back from his forehead. Rachel could imagine him raking it back with impatient fingers. And in the light from the open doorway it seemed to reflect the rich sheen of the black leather jacket that encased his broad shoulders.

He's quite splendid, Rachel decided. But definitely trouble.

'What circumstances?' she demanded again. 'And who are you?' she added. She already knew, of course, but he ought to have the manners to introduce himself!

He answered neither question. Instead he observed, 'I would never have guessed you were Emily's daughter.' As he spoke, he appeared to be studying Rachel every bit as thoroughly as she'd just studied him.

His eyes swept over her tall, shapely figure, dressed in a plain white T-shirt and blue Bermudas, pausing to examine her pale-skinned oval face, with its gentle rosebud mouth, tip-tilted nose and steady, slightly serious dark hazel eyes.

'You're not a bit like her.' His eyes drifted with a smile to the riot of flame-red corkscrew curls that tumbled to just below her shoulders. 'That hair, for example,' he observed, one eyebrow lifting. 'You definitely didn't get that from your mother.'

'I got it from my grandfather. My grandfather Bennet.'

Rachel smiled a small smile to herself as she said it. Throughout her twenty-four years her flaming red hair had always been a cause for comment—even among her own family, who were all utterly entranced by the mysterious fact that the famous Bennet hair had somehow skipped a generation, then reappeared only in her. Neither her two younger sisters nor any of her cousins had inherited it. Rachel had always considered herself rather lucky.

But such thoughts were far from her mind now as she looked into Claudio's face, over which a look of unrestrained appreciation was currently passing.

'I wonder why your mother never told me she had such a stunning daughter?' Claudio paused and smiled at her. '*Bellissima*,' he purred.

Instantly, warning bells were ringing in Rachel's head. Perhaps her mother hadn't been exaggerating, she was thinking, when she'd told her that not only was Dino's nephew the most unprincipled, unscrupulous bully imaginable, but a shameless, barefaced womaniser as well. Rachel had taken it with a pinch of salt. Her mother was inclined to be straitlaced and was prone at times to exaggeration. But now she found herself wondering if that last remark, which had appeared to be no more than an inoffensive compliment, had really been a prelude to some intended seduction. Claudio del'Angelo was in for a disappointment if it was.

Rachel threw him a discouraging look and demanded impatiently, 'Perhaps, if you don't mind, we could dispense with the frivolities and you could tell me instead the reason why you're here?'

She most definitely was not in the market for seduction and the sooner he realised that the better!

'There's really no point,' she added frostily, though frostiness normally wasn't Rachel's style at all, 'in the two of us wasting each other's time.'

'Indeed there isn't.' To Rachel's annoyance, he smiled. He simply found her frostiness amusing. Then the lightness left his expression and his tone grew grim again as he told her, 'I need, rather urgently, to speak to your mother's husband.'

He held her gaze, the black eyes narrowing. 'Have Dino and your mother gone out somewhere?' he demanded. 'I noticed there was no sign of their car outside.'

Now it was Rachel's turn to smile. 'Yes, you could say they've gone out. But it looks as though you've had a wasted journey.' As a frown touched his brow, she leaned lightly against the banisters and proceeded to elaborate with barely concealed relish, 'They've gone to Capri to visit friends.'

'To Capri?' Claudio's expression instantly darkened. Narrowed eyes, as sharp as bayonets, went piercing through her. 'Are you quite sure about that?' he demanded.

'Quite sure, I'm afraid. As I said, you've wasted your time. But if you want to leave a message I'll be happy to pass it on when they get back.'

Claudio didn't even wait for her to finish the sentence. She was barely halfway through it when he turned away brusquely.

'I need a drink,' he growled to no one in particular. Then, with a sharp click of heels against the polished hall tiles, he was heading with impatient strides for the drawing-room.

Damned cheek of him! Who did he think he was, treating this house as though it were his own, when the truth of the matter was he wasn't even welcome? Her mother, who, quite frankly, never had a good word to say for him, would be spitting furious, Rachel reflected, if she knew that the odious Claudio del'Angelo was at this moment in her drawing-room, casually pouring himself a drink!

Squaring her shoulders, she descended the final two steps of the staircase and proceeded across the hall with firm, determined strides. Well, she didn't want him around either and she would jolly well get rid of him—right now, before he had a chance to make himself at home!

But as she came to stand in the drawing-room doorway Claudio was already looking quite at home, seated in one of her mother's green chintz armchairs, cracking open a can of lager which he had evidently taken from the bar fridge and pouring its contents into a tall, straight-sided glass. He had removed his leather jacket, which now lay tossed across the sofa cushions, and his arms against the pushed-back sleeves of his pale blue shirt looked extraordinarily dark and muscular, she thought.

Rachel dismissed that thought instantly and, donning a fierce scowl, demanded, as she quickly raised her eyes to his face, 'Why are you here? What have you come for? From what I know about you, I can guess it's probably trouble.'

'And what do you know about me?'

'I know who you are.'

'Expecting me, were you?'

'No, as a matter of fact, I wasn't.'

'Then how come you so cleverly know who I am?' He laid aside the empty lager can and took a long, slow mouthful of his drink.

'I put two and two together. You said you wanted to see Dino. I assumed you were probably his nephew.'

As she'd spoken, Rachel had folded her arms across her chest and remained standing just inside the drawing-room doorway. She would not admit to him, she had decided, that she had recognised him from his photograph. She had no wish to flatter him with the admission that his face was so memorable. Instead she added in a tone that was far from flattering, 'Besides, I've been told a little about you. The way you came barging into the villa I just knew it couldn't possibly be anyone else.'

'So, I have a reputation for barging into people's houses, do I?' Claudio smiled with amusement as he leaned back and looked at her. 'I wonder how I managed to get a reputation like that?'

Rachel hesitated for a moment as the dark eyes held hers. While he'd been speaking, she'd been reflecting that he had the most melodious accent. Everything he said managed to sound like music. Just for a moment she'd forgotten how irritating he was.

But now, as he fixed her with those arrogant dark eyes of his, all her irritation came flooding back in an instant. She straightened her spine. 'That's not what I meant. You don't have a reputation for barging into people's houses. You just have a reputation for being—overbearing and bullying.'

She'd hesitated about being so frank—her natural English politeness!—but then she'd decided, why should I care about offending him? He's already offended me by barging in here in the first place!

And, besides, she knew perfectly well that he wouldn't be offended. It would take more than any puny insults she could come up with to offend a man of the consuming self-importance of Claudio del'Angelo!

She was right. Claudio didn't look offended in the slightest. On the contrary, he seemed to be enjoying this little verbal skirmish. The black eyes beneath the black brows were dancing with amusement.

'Overbearing and bullying?' he observed, taking another mouthful of his lager. 'I wonder who on earth could have called me that?'

Rachel said nothing. They'd been her mother's choice of words—though she could see for herself that her mother had been right. Overbearing and bullying were precisely what he was!

She sensed he knew what she was thinking—he certainly knew, she was sure of it, that it was her mother who had dubbed him overbearing and bullying!—but he continued to smile that arrogantly amused smile of his, quite clearly not bothered in the slightest.

Then he put to her, 'So, it would appear that we know what brings *me* here—I'm looking for trouble, as you so perceptively pointed out. But what about you?' He treated her to a narrow look. 'What brings Emily's daughter to the green hills of Tuscany?'

'I'm here on holiday. What else would I be doing?'

'I don't know what else . . . but I'm curious to find out.'

'Nothing else. Just a holiday. As I said.'

But even as she insisted, Rachel felt herself flushing beneath the ruthless scrutiny of that sharp, probing gaze. It was as though he could see inside her head and read all her secrets. As though he knew that this wasn't just a simple holiday; that there was something personal and very private that she was holding back.

But she had every right to keep her secrets. They were not for Claudio's ears. The traumas she'd come here to recover from were absolutely none of his business.

She took a deep breath and said again, firmly, 'Just a holiday.'

'I see.' He nodded, though his eyes were still sceptical. 'And have you come alone or did you bring a friend?'

'I came alone.'

'How odd.'

'There's nothing odd about it.'

'No, perhaps not—not if you were expecting to spend time with your mother. In which case your timing was rather bad, wouldn't you say?'

'What do you mean?' Though she was pretty sure she knew what he meant.

'Well, you tell me she and Dino have just gone off to Capri. I would say that was very bad timing indeed. Most unfortunate, particularly since you've obviously just arrived.'

He let his gaze drift for a moment over the pale skin of her face and arms. 'And you have just arrived, haven't you? You have that pale English look.'

'Yes. I have just arrived. A couple of days ago.' Rachel glanced down at her milk-white arms almost apologetically. 'I haven't had time to get a tan yet.'

'And you look beautiful without one.'

Again his eyes flitted over her, that warm look of appreciation flickering darkly in their depths. And, to her shame, Rachel very nearly blushed in response, unhinged for a moment by the sheer seductive power of him.

Yes, she found herself thinking, he was definitely an expert when it came to women. And it wasn't really hard to see why they fell. For there was something deeply alluring about the coal-black, long-lashed eyes and the way his wide mouth curved sensuously at the corners. Rachel found herself recalling some of the stories her mother had told her of the scores of women he'd seduced and ruined forever and found herself wondering if she'd been wise to tell him she was alone here.

She felt a rush of adrenalin. I'll fight him off with my bare hands if he comes anywhere near me! she promised herself.

But as he continued now there was no hint of seduction in his tone. Rather, there was a distinct edge of accusation.

'But we were talking, before we got side-tracked, of bad timing,' he reminded her, 'though I suspect there's rather more than just bad timing involved here... I would say it's really rather peculiar that your mother and her husband should go off to Capri and leave you all alone here virtually the minute you arrive. Unless, of course, there's some logic to it all that I'm unaware of?'

What was he getting at? Rachel had no idea. And though she too had thought it a little peculiar when her mother had announced on her very first night here that she and Dino had arranged to visit friends in Capri Rachel had no intention of admitting that to Claudio.

Instead she told him, defending her mother, 'It's not so strange, really. I came at very short notice. It's not surprising that my mother and Dino already had other things planned.'

'They could have taken you with them.' Claudio continued to look at her with that unsettlingly probing look in his eyes. 'Wouldn't that have been the normal thing? Unless, of course, there was some reason why you would want to stay on without them.'

'There was no reason.'

Rachel fended him off with her eyes. He was treading much too close to her secrets again—for the exodus to Capri had in fact suited her quite well. On her own here she had all the peace and quiet she needed to unwind. She was rather glad her mother hadn't invited her to go with them to Capri.

'I'm not a baby,' she assured Claudio. 'I can manage on my own. I'm a big girl, you know. I don't need my mother to look after me.'

As soon as she said that 'big girl' bit, she wished she hadn't. It had sparked a look of knowing amusement in his eyes. He was still smiling as he told her, 'I'm very glad to hear it—that you're capable of looking after yourself, that is.' He regarded her for a moment, then he raised his glass and drained it before holding it out to her with an arrogant, amused smile. 'Are you also good at taking care of your guests, I wonder? I wouldn't mind another lager.'

Damned impertinence! 'You're not my guest!' Rachel shot back at him. She refrained from adding that the only lager she was likely to provide him with was one poured over his arrogant head! 'And, since you've finished your lager, I suggest you leave now. I'm afraid I've had enough of answering questions. What my mother and Dino do is none of your business.'

'I'm afraid I'm making it my business. And I'm not leaving just yet.'

'Oh, yes, you are.' Rachel took a step towards him, half intending to snatch the empty lager glass from his hand, which was draped casually and irritatingly along the arm of the armchair. But she chickened out halfway. If she got that close, he might grab her. The very thought sent a shiver of pure horror down her spine.

He seemed to have guessed her intention and smiled at her now. 'Come on,' he said, taunting her. 'Come and take it. Then you can refill it from one of the cans you'll find in the fridge right there behind you.'

'I had no intention of refilling it. I was simply going to confiscate it. Just to let you know that you're really not welcome here.'

'And what stopped you?'

'My good manners.' Her tone was dark with irony. 'I decided to be polite and ask you again to leave.'

'I'll leave all right.' Claudio laid his glass on the floor beside him, causing a spurt of hope in her that he really was about to go. Then he sat back in his chair again, crushing that hope, and looked at her. 'Just as soon as you've answered a couple of questions.'

'I'm not answering any more questions. I've already told you that.' Rachel stuffed her hands mutinously into the pockets of her blue Bermudas and faced him with a look of exasperated annoyance. 'You know, you've really got a nerve,' she accused him, 'barging in here then proceeding to bombard me with questions!'

Claudio shrugged. 'I guess you'll just have to put that down to my overbearing and bullying nature.' He smiled for a moment, then his expression grew more serious again. 'And you really would be wise to co-operate,' he advised her. 'I'm not leaving until I have some answers.'

Rachel glared at him. It was unbearable the way he was sitting there, as though he had every right to be there, in her mother's green chintz armchair, his long jean-clad legs stretched out imperiously in front of him, black-shod feet crossed contemptuously at the ankles, every cat-supple line and angle of his body seeming to make some subtle statement of authority.

And now she was remembering something else her mother had told her.

'He's a big shot. He's only thirty-four, but he's one of the top architects in all Europe. And he likes to be treated like a big shot, too. Whatever Claudio del'Angelo says automatically goes.'

Rachel's instinctive reaction to someone like that was to cross them. She hated big shots and self-important bullies. But by crossing him she didn't seem to be making much headway. He really meant it; he wouldn't leave until she'd answered his questions.

And suddenly she was deeply anxious for him to be gone. There was something about his presence that made her uneasy. He was ruining her quiet little haven of tranquility, and totally upsetting her precious peace of mind.

She took a deep breath and made a decision. It might be in her own interests to be a little more co-operative. 'OK,' she told him, folding her arms across her chest. 'Go ahead and ask me whatever you want to know and I'll do my best to provide some answers.'

After all, she didn't have anything to hide, she told herself. He seemed to think there was something furtive going on, but he was absolutely wrong about that.

'That's more like it.' Claudio smiled with approval and leaned back more comfortably in his chair. Though there was still a shadow of distrust in his eyes. He probably thought everyone was a rogue like himself!

'So,' he continued, 'they've gone to Capri, you say... To visit friends... How long will they be gone?'

'I don't know exactly.' Her mother had been a bit vague about that. 'All they said was that they'd definitely be back before I left.'

'And when are you leaving?'

'I'm planning to stay for about three weeks.'

'About three weeks?' Claudio made a sharp clicking sound of disapproval. He did not look pleased in the slightest at this news. 'So it could be some time before your mother and Dino reappear.'

'Yes, I'm afraid it could.' Rachael found his displeasure warming. There was something deeply satisfying about thwarting this man.

'In that case, it looks as though I'll have to go and find them.' He eyed her questioningly. 'I presume you have the address of where they're staying?'

Rachel shook her head. 'No, I'm afraid I don't.' And, though she rather enjoyed the black look that touched his eyes at this further lack of information, it struck her that perhaps it was a genuine pity that she didn't know where her mother and Dino were staying. For she had a feeling that if she'd been able to produce an address Claudio might have climbed straight back on to his motorbike and left her in peace.

As it was, he proceeded to fix her with a dangerous look. 'You're absolutely sure about that?' he pressed her.

'Absolutely sure.'

'A phone number, then? They must have left you a phone number, at least.'

Again Rachel shook her head. 'My mother said she was going to. She said she would write it on the notepad in the kitchen . . .' Her voice tapered off, then she added with a shrug, 'But when I checked she hadn't. I guess she forgot.'

'I guess she did.' Claudio's tone was steely. He sat forward in his seat a little, narrowing his dark eyes at her. 'So, you have no address and no phone number. That's what you'd have me believe.' He smiled a grim smile, the dark eyes hooking into her. 'But at least you must know the name of the people they've gone to stay with?'

'I'm afraid I don't know that either.' It was suddenly beginning to strike Rachel that she really was lamentably ignorant about the whole thing. She dredged her brain for a moment, then smiled as she remembered. 'Franco and Maria . . . I think that's what they said.' She paused. 'Or maybe it was Franca and Mario. I'm sorry,' she added, unable to resist a smile.

Claudio did not smile back. Instead he delivered a look like thunder. 'And this Franca and Mario . . . or Franco and Maria . . . Would you happen to know their surname?'

Rachel sighed. 'I'm sorry. They didn't mention any surnames.'

For a long, icy moment Claudio said nothing. Then he fixed her with a look that seemed to skewer right through her. 'Are you telling me the truth,' he demanded evenly, 'or are you lying?'

'Why should I lie? I have no reason to lie.'

'I think you have.' There was an edge of impatience to his tone. 'In fact, I think that what you've just told me is an entire pack of lies.'

Rachel bridled at that. 'I don't like being called a liar! I have nothing to hide and neither have my mother and Dino! If I knew where they were, or whom they were staying with, I'd tell you.'

'Would you? Even if Dino and Emily had told you not to?'

'But they didn't tell me not to. And why on earth would they, anyway?'

'Perhaps because they'd rather I didn't find them.'

'Well, I can sympathise with that!' Rachel couldn't resist it. Then she quickly assured him, 'But they didn't tell me not to tell you. And anyway how could I? I don't know myself!'

She let out a sharp, impatient breath. 'Look, what's going on here? You talk as though there's some sort of conspiracy. Well, there's not, I can assure you. It's all very straightforward. They've gone to Capri to see some friends and simply forgot to leave their number——'

She broke off as Claudio suddenly began to rise to his feet, his tall, powerful frame unfolding threateningly from the armchair.

'No,' he was saying, 'I don't think that's how it is. I don't think that's how it is at all.'

He took a step towards her, his hands in his trouser pockets, his dark eyes lazily flaying her face. 'Shall I tell you how I think it is?' He paused and frowned down at her. 'Unless, of course, you'd like to tell me first?'

Rachel's mouth had gone quite dry. He looked like a panther about to pounce. She licked her dry lips. 'I don't know how it is... I mean, it's how I already told you...'

He came to a stop right in front of her, so close that she could feel the warmth of him wrap itself round her and hold her there like a prisoner.

'This is how I think it is,' he started to tell her. 'I think that what's happened is that they've run off to Capri, leaving you here to hold the fort...'

'What do you mean "hold the fort"? What do you mean "run off"?'

Suddenly, Rachel could feel the claws of panic inside her. The way he was standing over her was really quite worrying, and the things he was saying were simply confusing her. All at once, she was finding it difficult to breathe.

'Wh-what on earth do you think they've run away from?' she stuttered, hastily taking an unsteady step back.

Claudio smiled then, though it was a smile that held little humour. Then, taking another step towards her, once more closing the gap between them, he answered very simply, 'I think they've run away from me.'

'You?'

Rachel swallowed, feeling as though she was choking as his heat and the mingled scents of him seemed to press against her. She blinked at him as he told her, 'You see, they knew I was on my way here. I warned them several days ago of my intentions. They knew what I was planning to do.'

'What were you planning to do?'

Rachel tried to step away again, but her heel had caught on the edge of the carpet. Desperately, she struggled to free it, only half listening as Claudio enlightened her.

'I was planning to evict them. To throw them out of this house. You see, I've had more than enough of their tricks and their dishonesty.' He smiled a sinister smile. 'I'm afraid it's come-uppance time for dear Uncle Dino and his wife.'

As he paused for breath, his eyes grew even harder. 'But it would appear they've done a runner,' he continued in a harsh tone, 'and left you to hold the fort in their absence...'

It was in that moment that Rachel almost managed to free her foot. But in her panic she moved too quickly and stumbled awkwardly, her flailing arms colliding with Claudio's ribcage as she fought to stop herself from falling.

But there was no danger of her falling, for Claudio had caught her by the wrist and was snatching her to him as though she were a lifeless puppet.

'And finding you here is a most interesting development,' he purred. 'One that I definitely hadn't been expecting...' As he looked down into her face, his eyes burned like firebrands. 'So now what I have to decide is what I'm going to do with you...'

CHAPTER TWO

RACHEL froze, her heart thundering wildly inside her, her body on fire where it was pressed up against Claudio's. And for a moment she had the feeling of having totally lost control. She felt routed and utterly at his mercy.

But an instant later, with desperate strength, she had snatched herself free from him and was gathering together her scattered composure. She rounded on him, hazel eyes flashing with anger.

'So, you're wondering what you're going to do with me, are you? Well, let me tell you, you're going to do nothing!' She faced him squarely, hands on hips, tossing back her hair from her still flushed face. 'Let's get that clear right from the start!'

Claudio had taken a step back and was surveying her now with an expression of mingled admiration and amusement. 'You're a fighter, I see. A real red-haired fury. I'll try to remember that in future.'

'Yes, kindly make sure you do!'

Rachel was breathing heavily as she continued to face him with anger-filled eyes. She'd never thought of herself as a fighter. She certainly didn't go looking for fights, and she'd never fought with Mark once in the two years she'd known him! But Claudio del'Angelo was a whole different kettle of fish from quiet, unassuming, civilised Mark, and there was no way she was going to allow him to walk all over her!

'So, if you're looking for someone to bully,' she warned him, 'you'd better look for someone else!'

'Bully you? Was I really bullying you?' Claudio feigned a look of shock, as though such an accusation were quite outrageous. 'All I was doing was simply trying to make a point.' He paused and with a wicked smile held her eyes for a moment. 'And, if you recall, you were the one who started getting physical first.'

'I didn't get physical. I simply lost my balance. My heel was caught in the carpet and I couldn't get away from you.'

Her stomach tightened as she said it, for suddenly she was recalling the powerful, frantic way she had reacted to his nearness. It had been out of all proportion. What had come over her?

She licked her dry lips and shifted as she looked at him. 'I had no desire to get physical. I simply wanted to escape.'

'Escape? Why, what on earth did you think I was going to do to you?' Claudio raised one strongly curved, amused dark eyebrow.

'I had no idea.' Rachel met his gaze steadily. 'But I didn't plan on staying around to find out.'

Claudio shook his head at that and held her eyes for a moment. Then his face broke into a smile as understanding dawned.

'Oh, dear,' he said. 'What has Emily been telling you about me? Has she been telling you that I'm some kind of mad rapist or something?'

'Not exactly.'

But Rachel dropped her eyes as she answered. For her mother's lurid tales of his ferocious carnal appetites had been very much in her mind only a moment ago when she had suddenly found herself locked in his clutches. Who knew what to expect of a man with a reputation like his?

Still smiling and shaking his head, Claudio began to turn away, heading for the bar fridge in the corner. He pulled open the door and pulled out a can of lager, then snapped back the ring-pull and took a mouthful from the can before crossing to retrieve his glass from where he had put it down and emptying the frothing contents of the can into the glass.

Raising one eyebrow, he glanced at Rachel. 'Your mother thinks I'm a sex maniac.' His lips curled wickedly at the corners. Evidently, he found this assessment amusing. 'Is that what you think too?' he demanded curiously.

'I really have no idea. I don't even know you.'

Rachel's tone was clipped. This was not a topic she wished to pursue. It made her feel distinctly uncomfortable.

'But then, your mother tends to be a bit puritanical.' Claudio sat down casually on the arm of the armchair and took a mouthful of his lager. 'It doesn't take much to shock your mother.'

'Is that a fact?'

'And how about you?'

'How about me?'

'Are you as easily shocked as your mother?'

'Maybe by your standards I am.'

Rachel glared at him disapprovingly, resisting the urge to fold her arms across her chest. That would definitely make her look a little uptight and puritanical, and what she wanted was to look as cool and in command of the situation as he was.

He seemed to consider her answer. Then he demanded to know, 'So, is that what you are? A puritanical little schoolteacher?'

'As I said, maybe by your standards.' Rude pig, she was thinking. She felt like punching him on the nose.

Perhaps he knew that, for he continued with his baiting.

'I wonder, are all English women puritanical?'

'Why don't you go over to England and find out for yourself?' Right now, right this minute. Rachel felt like adding. She would gladly have made a contribution to his plane fare just to be rid of him.

'Oh, I've been, but I only stayed for a couple of weeks. Not enough time to enjoy a very large sample.'

'No? You surprise me. I thought two weeks would have been ample time. At the rate you go through women, you ought to have managed a couple of dozen, at least.'

It had been a reflex action. It had come out before she could stop it. But as soon as she'd said it Rachel felt totally appalled at herself. She pursed her lips, as though to stop any more folly pouring out of them, and abruptly folded her arms across her chest.

'A couple of dozen in two weeks? So, that's what Emily's been telling you. Well, I have to admit that's pretty flattering, though perhaps just a bit of an overestimate.' Claudio swirled the lager in his glass for a moment, his eyes fixed on Rachel's face and dancing with amusement. 'You see, on the whole, I tend to prefer quality to quantity. Making love's a bit like playing a Mozart concerto: it's not nearly so pleasurable if you try to rush it.' He took another mouthful of his lager and enquired, 'Wouldn't you agree?'

Rachel was trying to control the anger that was surging through her. By way of a response she simply pursed her lips tighter.

'Does that mean that you don't agree—or that you have no opinion?' He swirled his glass some more, his dark eyes laughing at her.

'It means I don't wish to pursue this conversation.'

She'd meant that to sound scathing, but it came out sounding prim. And how prim she must look, she suddenly thought with annoyance, standing there with her arms folded like barbed wire across her chest and her mouth pursed in disapproval like some outraged virgin.

She almost smiled at that thought. After all, she was a virgin—a species a man like Claudio doubtless rarely encountered!—though, for all that, she was in no way, shape or form a prude. Which was just as well, she decided, with a reprobate like Claudio to contend with!

But then he shrugged. 'OK. Let's change the subject. Though I suspect you won't get much enjoyment out of this one either.' As he spoke, his expression radically altered, all traces of amusement abruptly gone. 'If you recall, we were discussing the whereabouts of Dino and your mother.'

'I thought we'd exhausted that subject? I told you I didn't know where they were.'

In spite of her impatient tone, Rachel felt only relief at this change of tack. This was equally thorny, but less hazardous ground. She had no problem at all in coping with his hostility. It was that other, seductive side of him that she found unsettling.

'I know what you told me, but I didn't necessarily believe you.' His eyes ground into her, as hard as granite. 'I was hoping that this time you might tell me the truth.'

'The truth is what I've already told you. I'm afraid I can't improve on it.' Rachel looked back at him, as before, thoroughly enjoying thwarting him. Then, remembering something, she narrowed her eyes at him. 'What did you mean when you said you'd come here to evict my mother and Dino? How can you evict someone from their own house?'

'You can't.'

'That's what I would have thought.'

'And you would have been right.' With a thoughtful look, Claudio swirled the lager in his glass, glancing down for a moment into the pale froth that rose up. Then he raised his eyes to Rachel's. 'But this is not their house, you see. This house, as it happens, belongs to me.'

'To you?'

'Didn't they tell you?'

'That this is your house? I was under the impression that the house was Dino's.' And she'd been under that impression because her mother had said so. 'I find what you're claiming quite extraordinary,' she added.

'No doubt you do, but it remains the truth, for all that.' Claudio tilted his head and drained the lager in his glass, then laid the empty glass on a nearby table. 'So, you see, that explains how I have the power to evict them.'

'If it's true.'

'It's true.'

'So how come they're living here?'

'They're living here because Dino's supposed to be buying the house from me. That was the plan. That was what we agreed. I have a new house and no longer need this one. So when I moved out I let them move in.'

'Only now you've changed your mind?' That sounded typical. 'Suddenly you don't want them staying here any more?' Rachel cast him a frankly disapproving look. 'Is this because you've fallen out with your uncle?'

'Perhaps it's the other way round. Perhaps I've fallen out with my uncle because of the irresponsible way he's handled the purchase of the house.'

He seemed about to add something else, then paused with a thoughtful look to glance for a moment through the window across the room at the vista of green hills and sapphire-blue sky. And, as Rachel followed his gaze she felt a sharp stab of frustration as she compared the peaceful scene beyond the window with the tense, charged atmosphere in the room.

Peace and tranquility were what she'd come here searching for. And they were here, within her grasp,

They were all around her. But this wretched man had come and snatched them from her and was insisting on embroiling her in his petty disputes. She glared at him resentfully as he turned back to her and continued, 'I don't know how much you know, so I won't go into details. But let's just say that my uncle owes me a great deal of money. A very great deal. A debt he seems reluctant to honour. So I've decided it's time that something was done.'

This couldn't be true. He had to be inventing this, making Dino out to be the villain when the villain was really him!

'You mean you'd evict them just because Dino's missed a few payments on the house?' Rachel was shocked but not particularly surprised at his callousness. 'With relatives like you Dino certainly doesn't need any enemies.'

Claudio smiled at that. Then he told her, 'On the contrary, he's lucky I've been so patient with him so far.' His smile widened as Rachel pulled a frankly disbelieving face. Claudio patient? she was thinking. That was a good one. She'd be more likely to believe that cauliflowers could sing!

'Also, however,' he added, 'my patience has run out.'

'So, now you're going to run them out of their home? I think that's disgraceful. Where would they go?'

Claudio looked about as concerned as a rhinoceros with a bee sting. 'I'm afraid,' he informed her coldly, 'that is not my problem.' He leaned against the back of the green chintz armchair and studied her in silence for a moment. Then he smiled. 'My problem appears to be you.'

'Me? I fail to see why I'm any problem of yours.'

As she said it, Rachel felt a tingle of alarm down her spine. Hadn't he been saying something of this nature when he'd suddenly grabbed her earlier? She was extremely glad she was standing a safe distance away now.

She demanded, 'What has any of this to do with me?'

'Quite a lot, it seems to me.'

'Kindly explain.'

'Do I really need to?' Claudio's dark eyes held hers. 'Are you really as innocent as you would have me believe?'

Rachel sighed. 'So, we're back to the conspiracy theory, I see. You think I'm involved in some elaborate set-up to stop you throwing my mother and Dino out of the house. But you can't throw them out, anyway. They've gone to Capri!'

'Leaving you to hold the fort.'

'Hold the fort?'

'Protect their belongings.'

'What do you mean, protect their belongings?' Then she threw him a shocked look as she put two and two together. 'You mean you were planning to remove their possessions?'

'Quite frankly, I would have preferred it if they'd done it themselves—as I told my uncle last time we spoke on the phone. But I also told him that if they failed to move out I'd send a van round to do the job for them.'

'You mean that's why you're here? To throw out their belongings? Well, I'm sorry if my being here is spoiling your fun.'

Claudio simply smiled in the face of her irony. He didn't care that she thought him an absolute toad.

'Not fun, exactly,' he corrected her in a mild tone. 'I wouldn't quite go as far as that.'

'Wouldn't you? I think you're selling yourself short. I think throwing people and their belongings out of their houses is probably precisely the sort of thing you enjoy.'

Rachel glared at him, suddenly bristling with outrage. Her mother and Dino had made a beautiful home here, one that they obviously both cared for very much, and Claudio del'Angelo was planning to rip it all apart, just because Dino had defaulted on a couple of payments! It was shocking. Barbaric. The man had no heart.

'If you want to know what I think, I think it's a disgrace.'

'And is that why you're here—because you think it's a disgrace? Is that why you've been planted here—in order to try and stop me?'

'I haven't been planted here!' There he went again with his talk of conspiracies! 'And anyway, how could I possibly stop you?' she demanded. 'I suspect it would take more than one ill-equipped female to stop you doing something you'd set your mind on!'

'You're not so ill-equipped. Quite the contrary, I'd say.'

As he smiled at her, his eyes never flickered from her face. But Rachel couldn't help feeling as though they were travelling all over her, caressing the full, soft swell of her breasts and the womanly curves of her hips and thighs.

I'm going paranoid, she thought. I'm getting obsessed with this seduction stuff. What's got into me? she wondered. I'm not normally like this!

She tilted her chin at him and pulled herself together. 'We seem to be straying from the point again,' she told him. 'We were talking about your plan to empty my mother's house——'

'That's right. And you were saying how hard it would be to stop me doing something I'd set my mind on.' He held her eyes and smiled a bold smile. 'You're a good judge of character. It would be very hard indeed. When I set my mind on something, ten times out of ten I get it.'

And again Rachel wondered if it was just her imagination as a glint of warning seemed to touch his eyes, making his immodest claim sound like a declaration of intent. If I were to decide I wanted you, it seemed to warn, you wouldn't stand a chance.

Whether it had been her imagination or not, Rachel felt a flush round her neck. Something deep and secret had stirred within her. Horror—outrage—she quickly told herself. She would die before she would ever allow him to lay a hand on her!

Then she gave herself a shake—damned man, what was he doing to her?—and, snatching back her poise, she turned with a flourish to wave a mock-magnanimous hand round the room.

'Well, go ahead and empty the house, if that's what you're here for. As I've said, I can't stop you. And I can assure you I haven't been planted here to try.'

Claudio regarded her for a moment, as though considering her challenge. 'Maybe not,' he conceded at last. 'Maybe they thought I was bluffing. Or maybe they thought I'd be too polite to throw out their guest.'

'Then they, it would seem, are very *bad* judges of character.' Rachel barely managed to suppress a contemptuous guffaw. 'I suspect that throwing me out along with the furniture would simply add to your enjoyment.' She tossed him a gritty look. 'So, are you going to throw me out? Would you like me to go and pack right away?'

Claudio said nothing for a moment. He rose slowly to his feet, then crossed to the nearby sofa to retrieve his leather jacket. And, just for a moment, a shaft of sunlight from the window made his hair gleam like polished ebony as it glanced across his head and shoulders and fixed his strong, handsome profile in a striking silhouette. And as she watched him, reflecting that he really was extraordinarily good-looking, it struck Rachel that it was a genuine pity he was such a skunk underneath.

Slinging the jacket over his shoulder, he turned to face her. 'That won't be necessary,' he said.

Rachel felt a quick dart of triumph, though she tried not to show it. Was he actually about to admit defeat and go?

It seemed so. He said softly, 'No, I'm not going to throw you out. I've decided that would probably be counter-productive.'

Rachel was not about to argue. As he started to walk towards her, casually slipping his free hand into his trouser pocket, she decided to offer some encouragement in the face of this happy turn-around.

'If they get in touch, I'll find out where they are and let you know. Just leave me your phone number before you go.'

'How very co-operative of you.'

'There's a pad around here somewhere.' She glanced quickly round her, then her eyes fell on the scribbling pad by the phone behind her. She reached out and snatched it up, along with the pen that lay beside it. Then she held them out to Claudio. 'You can write the number down here.'

But Claudio ignored the pad and pen as he came to a stop right in front of her. Instead he proceeded to ask her a question that completely floored her.

'Which of the spare bedrooms are you using?'

Rachel faltered for a moment, wondering what on earth he was up to and forcing herself to resist the urge to jump back away from him. Then she told him, 'Since you ask, I'm in the bedroom at the front.'

Claudio nodded. 'OK.' Then he swept past her, still ignoring the pad and pen she held out. In the doorway, he paused and informed her over his shoulder, 'In that case, I'll move into the spare bedroom at the back.'

'You'll *what*?'

Rachel was aware that her jaw had dropped open. As he headed across the hall, totally ignoring her shocked expression, she hurried after him, demanding an explanation.

'I don't think I heard you right. What did you say? Would you mind repeating that, please?'

'Not at all.'

Claudio was striding through the still open front door, pulling on his leather jacket as he headed for the black and silver motorbike. A moment later he was climbing aboard.

He flicked her an arrogant look. 'I said I'll move into the back bedroom.' The he smiled as he kicked the starter and added over the roar of the engine, 'We'll discuss it when I get back. I have a plan, you see.'

'A plan? What plan? Look, I hope this is some kind of joke!'

But Rachel might have saved her breath for all the effect her protests were having. For as she stood there, fuming, he was roaring off down the drive, scattering gravel in all directions.

There was always a chance, Rachel told herself once she'd calmed down a little, that he'd been bluffing and in fact had no intention of moving in.

Perhaps he'd just wanted to ruffle her feathers, to scare her into co-operating with him and telling him where her mother and Dino were. For it was quite clear that he was not convinced that she had no idea.

It was also quite clear that he was definitely after them. So, was it true that they'd gone to Capri to escape him, as he'd suggested? It was all very weird. Rachel didn't know what to believe. But something— and something rather unpleasant—was obviously going on.

Rachel racked her brains to remember something her mother might have told her in one of her recent letters or phone calls. But she could think of nothing that would throw any light on the situation. And nothing had been said either during the short time they'd spent together before her mother and Dino's departure for Capri—only the usual stuff she'd heard before about that 'odious, bullying Claudio'.

But then, they hadn't really had much time for confidences. Rachel hadn't even had a chance to mention Mark's marriage proposal. Which was probably a good thing, Rachel had decided. Since her mother's blissful marriage to local businessman Dino just two years ago—after what had been, Rachel knew, a long and lonely widowhood—she'd turned into a somewhat aggressive supporter of marriage and might very well have tried to persuade her daughter to change her mind. She wouldn't have succeeded, of course, but she'd have had a jolly good try. These days she just wanted to see everyone with a wedding-ring!

Still, that was not what was concerning Rachel now as she paced round the villa, unable to relax, unable to settle. What she really felt like doing was having a swim in the pool or stretching out on a sunbed with a book for a while. But how could she do that when at any moment Claudio might show up? It was just impossible to relax with his threat hanging over her.

For if he did show up she wanted to be on hand to confront him and demand in no uncertain terms his immediate departure. And any confrontation with Claudio would be much easier to handle in an upright position and with all her clothes on!

At least he didn't let her stew for very long.

Just over an hour later, Rachel heard the roar of a motorbike coming down the villa driveway. She rushed to the front door and flung it open, and sure enough it was Claudio, looking as arrogant as ever and armed this time with a bulging leather holdall.

Not only was it clear that he intended moving in, it would appear that he had prepared himself for a lengthy sojourn.

Over my dead body, Rachel thought to herself in fury, planting herself like a boulder at the top of the front-door steps. He's crazy if he thinks I'm going to allow that!

'Where do you think you're going?' As he headed towards her with that arrogant smile that infuriated her so profoundly, Rachel thrust back her shoulders, her arms folded across her chest, and tilted back her head so that she was looking down her nose at him. 'Kindly don't come another step nearer,' she warned him. 'This is my mother's house and I don't want you here.'

'Yes, I can see that.' He had come to a halt in front of her. His eyes danced over her face for a moment, clearly highly amused by her fierce expression. But though his tone was light it held an edge of warning as he added, 'But, I'm afraid, you have one essential detail wrong. The house belongs to me, as I've already explained. So kindly move aside and let me past.'

'No.'

'No?'

'That's right. No. I won't allow it. Maybe—though I doubt it—this house does belong to you, but it's still

my mother's home and you have no right to move
in.'

'You think not, do you? Well, let's argue about that
inside.' Claudio shifted suddenly and took a step
towards her.

Instantly, Rachel swung her arms wide to bar his
way. 'No!' she protested again. 'You're not coming
in!'

Her legs were planted wide, her body stiff and for-
bidding. He'd have to lift her up bodily if he wanted
to get past her, and if he so much as tried to lay a
hand on her she'd fight him off with all her strength.
She'd kick and scream and beat him with her fists.
She glared at him warningly. 'Don't,' she advised.
'Don't try any rough stuff or you'll be sorry, I
promise!'

Claudio regarded her for a moment with apparent
interest. Then he smiled a half-smile. 'OK. No rough
stuff.'

Then he just stood there watching her as she glared
back at him belligerently, her breasts thrust out
towards him beneath the taut lines of her T-shirt.

Perhaps he thinks he can intimidate me into moving
aside, she thought. Well, he's in for a surprise. I don't
intimidate so easily. I'll continue to stand here until
my arms drop off!

But that was when he did something totally
unexpected.

Suddenly, before she could do a single thing about
it, he was leaning towards her, slipping one arm
around her waist and bending down to deliver her a
kiss on the lips.

Rachel was so taken aback, she was instantly paralysed. As his mouth pressed down on hers, firm and warm and sensuous, for a moment she was convinced she must be dreaming. Surely this couldn't be happening? Surely he wouldn't have the nerve? And if it was happening, surely she wouldn't just be standing here letting it?

But it was real. It was happening. And she wasn't doing a thing to stop it.

Only because she couldn't. She felt a sudden rush inside her as she was aware that her stomach had turned all liquid and heavy. And her mouth felt as though an electric current was passing through it. Prickling. Tingling. Deliciously burning. All at once she hardly seemed to be breathing any more.

Do something! she kept telling herself through all these dizzy sensations. But what could she do? She was quite incapable of moving a muscle.

And then as suddenly as it had descended on her the whirlwind abated. As she continued to stand there, transfixed, like a mummy, Claudio detached his lips from hers and released his hold on her. Then, with a light, amused smile, he stepped away.

Rachel heard him say, 'Come inside and join me and I'll tell you all about this plan I have in mind.'

Then he was stepping past her and disappearing into the hall.

For a moment Rachel continued to stand where she was. She was aware that her arms had dropped limply to her sides and that her poor, startled heart was still thundering inside her. She shook herself mentally in an effort to regain sanity. What had happened to her?

she thought despairingly. Why had she allowed him to do that? It was a disgrace. She ought to be ashamed of herself. She had just stood there without a protest.

And now he was inside. Just like that, he had tricked her. How he must be laughing at her. How clever he must be feeling.

She turned on her heel angrily. Well, it wasn't over yet. He had managed to trick his way in, but she could still throw him out—and warn him never to try a trick like that again!

Propelled by her growing fury, she marched through the doorway and headed across the tiled hall to the drawing-room, half expecting to see him sitting in one of her mother's green chitz armchairs pouring himself a glass of lager. But there was no sign of him there. He must have gone upstairs.

Rachel almost ran up the stairs and strode quickly along the corridor until she reached the bedroom at the back. It was as though she needed to hurry to keep up the pitch of her anger. She was afraid of losing momentum if she slowed down.

The door was half-open. She tapped on it impatiently. 'Are you in there? I'd like a word, if you don't mind.' Then, before he could reply, she was pushing the door open. 'We have some unfinished business——' she started to say.

The words turned to bricks in her mouth. She stopped short, her face burning. For he was standing by the window, stripped to the waist and quite clearly on the point of removing his lower garments as well.

His hand on the silver buckle of his tan leather belt, Claudio turned unhurriedly to face her. 'Unfinished business, you say?' He smiled at her wickedly. 'You surprise me. I hadn't realised you'd be quite so eager.' With the lift of one dark eyebrow, he beckoned her inside. 'But if you insist I'd be more than happy to oblige.'

Rachel glared at him, but it was herself she was really annoyed with. Just for a moment, as she'd looked at him, she'd been aware of the cool scent of him that still seemed to linger about her body, and of the way her mouth still burned as though stuck with hot needles. Just for a moment she'd felt that disgraceful paralysis of before.

'No, thank you.' She remained standing stiffly in the doorway, her expression reflecting the distaste in her voice. 'By unfinished business I meant I haven't agreed to your staying here. So please don't bother getting too settled in.'

She avoided looking at the leather holdall that lay unzipped on the floor and at the assortment of shirts and things strewn across the bed. Perhaps, it occurred to her, she was a little late with her warning. He already seemed to have made himself pretty much at home.

At any rate, he blithely ignored her admonition.

'I thought I would just go for a quick swim,' he told her, releasing his leather belt from the belt-loops of his jeans and tossing the belt on to the bed beside the shirts. 'Then you and I can have our little chat. In the meantime, why don't you change into your swimsuit and come and join me?' His hand was on the waistband of his jeans. 'There's plenty of room in the pool for two.'

Rachel heard the last part of that final sentence through the wooden panels of the door. She had no desire, she told herself, to be subjected to the depraved spectacle of Claudio del'Angelo displaying his wares. And as she stomped off down the corridor, belatedly realising that she had omitted to warn him never to try kissing her again, she simply ignored the amused chuckle that drifted out through the door.

To Rachel's furious annoyance, he spent nearly an hour in the pool. She sat on the kitchen patio and watched him, seething, as he executed one effortless length after another, cutting through the turquoise water as cleanly as a seal.

But at last he was lifting himself out on to the poolside, all glistening sinews and dripping wet hair, totally unaware that Rachel was watching him as he proceeded to open up one of the sun umbrellas and stretch himself out on the sunbed in the shade.

Rachel seethed some more from her chair on the patio. She'd been hoping that he might have the decency to go and get dressed so that they could have their little chat in a civilised manner. She might have guessed that that was too much to expect.

Well, she wasn't going to wait forever. She rose to her feet angrily and made her way across the patio towards the pool. At the end of his sunbed she came to a halt and glared down at him. But instead of launching straight into her little diatribe, as she had intended, she found herself hesitating just for a second.

He was lying with his eyes closed, his hands behind his head, and he really made quite an impressive spectacle. Rachel let her eyes travel over him. He had a magnificent body—lean and hard and perfectly proportioned. She had rarely seen a man quite so beautifully built.

'Instead of just standing there, why don't you sit down and join me?'

Rachel flushed crimson as he spoke. So he had known she was standing watching him! And she cursed herself again. What was wrong with her? Why did she keep allowing herself to be wrong-footed like this?

As he opened his eyes to look at her, she tore her gaze away and pretended to look round for another sunbed for herself. There was one right behind her. She reached for it gratefully and pulled it into the shade beside Claudio's, but not too close.

'Why didn't you join me in the pool? What's the matter, don't you swim?' He had pulled himself up a little so that he could see her better. 'It's beautifully cool in there. You really ought to try it.'

'Yes, I swim, but I'll try it later, thank you.'

Once you've gone, Rachel added silently as she seated herself opposite him on her sunbed.

He regarded her with interest. 'You're wise to stay in the shade. Fair skin like yours burns very easily. You'll have to take a great deal of care.'

Rachel already knew that. With her pale redhead's skin she always rationed her exposure to the sun very carefully. But she didn't need lectures on skincare from Claudio del'Angelo. And anyway she hadn't joined him to indulge in idle talk.

She cast him an impatient look. 'I don't know what you think you're doing here. It's really quite pointless, your going to all the trouble of moving in. I don't know where they are and, as I've already told you, if I find out I'll get in touch and let you know immediately.' *After warning them that you're after them, of course,* she added silently.

Then she took a deep breath and demanded with angry feeling, 'So, why don't you do me a favour and just pack up your bag and leave?'

'Oh, don't worry, I will. All in good time.' Her hostility bounced off him like raindrops off a window. Then he smiled at her and let his dark eyes rove over her face. 'But first I have something else in mind.'

'This plan you spoke about?' Rachel's tone was disparaging. She really wasn't interested in hearing about his plan. But all the same it was perfectly clear that he was planning to tell her anyway, so she pulled a bored face and demanded, 'And what plan might this be?'

Claudio took a moment to answer. His dark eyes continued to watch her and there was something in their expression that made Rachel's skin tingle.

Then he smiled and, quite straightforwardly, as though he were offering her a slice of toast, he told her, 'My plan is that you and I should become lovers.'

CHAPTER THREE

'I *BEG* your pardon?'

Rachel nearly fell off her sunbed. Had the wretched man taken complete leave of his senses?

She thinned her lips at him. 'That's quite outrageous! Where do you get the nerve to make a suggestion like that?'

Quite unconcerned by her fury, Claudio actually had the gall to laugh. 'Why?' he demanded, smiling at her. 'Don't you fancy the idea of us becoming lovers?'

'Fancy the idea? *Fancy* the idea?' Rachel's hazel eyes were popping out of her head. 'You're a maniac,' she told him, wondering if she should end this conversation immediately and just get up and go while the going was good—though what she really felt like doing, if only she'd had the strength, was picking him up bodily and flinging him into the swimming-pool. Though there'd be scant satisfaction in that. He could swim like a fish.

She glared at him. 'My mother was right. You're an absolute disgrace.'

Claudio leaned back on his sunbed and nodded at that. 'I'm glad you've brought your mother into the conversation,' he told her. 'You see, it was because of your mother that I made the suggestion in the first place.'

'It was because of my mother that you just suggested we become lovers?' Rachel eyed him, her expression one of total perplexity. 'Why?' she demanded with irony. 'Were you under the impression that she might approve?'

She smiled at the madness of the very idea. Her poor mother would be even more appalled than she was!

But Claudio was shaking his head. 'Quite the contrary,' he was telling her. 'I suggested it precisely because I know your mother would have a fit.'

Rachel frowned at him. 'And why would you want my mother to have a fit?'

Claudio held up one hand. 'Ah, now we're getting to the heart of the matter.' Then he pulled himself up to face her more squarely. And suddenly he smiled. 'Oh, by the way,' he told her, 'I seem to have omitted to make one point clear... I was only suggesting that we *pretend* to be lovers.'

'Pretend?'

'You look disappointed.'

'I look nothing of the sort!' Rachel felt herself colour at the very suggestion. 'If I was looking anything, I can assure you, it was heartily relieved. Not,' she added hurriedly, 'that it makes any difference. I have no intention of pretending such a thing either.'

But, as though she hadn't spoken, Claudio was continuing with wicked enjoyment, 'To have suggested that we become lovers for real at this point would have been just a little premature.'

Just a little premature! The shameless vanity of the man!

'Not so much premature, more downright prepos-
terous!' Rachel was quick to put him right. 'Just as
your suggestion that we pretend is also quite prepos-
terous.' She frowned into his face. In spite of her sense
of outrage, she was curious to know what lay behind
his mad suggestion. 'Why on earth would I want to
pretend such an unpalatable thing?'

Claudio ignored the insult. 'Because,' he told her,
'that's the only way you're going to get rid of me.'

Rachel was totally lost now. 'What are you talking
about? Why should that be the only way I'm going
to get rid of you?'

It was obvious that Claudio was enjoying her total
bafflement. He sat back on his sunbed and watched
her for a moment. Then he asked her a question. 'How
would your mother react if she got to hear that you
and I were having an affair?'

Well, that was an easy one. 'As you said, she'd have
a fit.'

'And, after she'd finished having her fit, what do
you suppose she'd do next?'

'She'd probably come steaming back here and
threaten you with severe physical damage.'

Rachel smiled as she said it, remembering how,
some time ago, her mother had described in one of
her letters what she would do if she were the mother
of one particular young female who'd currently been
seen in Claudio's company. 'I'd have his guts for
garters. I'd tear him limb from limb.' As the mother
of three daughters she'd clearly felt strongly. 'I
wouldn't let him within a mile of any daughter of
mine!' she'd declared.

Claudio was watching her. 'I can see the prospect of my being done severe physical damage appeals to you.'

'Let's say it doesn't exactly displease me.' It's no more than you deserve, she thought. Though it also occurred to her that Claudio would not make an easy victim. In fact, it was hard to think of Claudio making any kind of victim at all.

That rather spoiled her enjoyment. She grew more sober again. 'So, why would you want my mother to come gunning for you?' she asked him. 'Do you enjoy upsetting people's mothers?'

'You're missing the point.' Claudio shook his head at her. 'The point is, as you said, that she'd come hotfooting straight back here—with Uncle Dino right behind her, naturally.' He smiled. 'Since you're refusing to tell me where they've gone, that would save me the trouble of having to hang around here and prise it out of you.'

'Boy, you're tricky.' Rachel smiled at him dubiously, not quite sure how impressed she ought to be by his deviousness. For even she could see that it was a pretty clever plan. One whiff of an affair between herself and Claudio and her mother would definitely be back here like a shot. 'It takes a certain sort of mind to think up a plot like that,' she observed.

'Thank you.' Claudio smiled. 'I accept the compliment.' Though he knew perfectly well that Rachel had intended no compliment. Then he raised one dark eyebrow at her. 'So? Are you agreeable?'

Rachel's own eyebrows lifted in a display of mock-astonishment.

'You mean I actually get to have some say in the matter?'

'Of course you do. After all, I'd need your co-operation.'

'Good. In that case, the answer's no.'

'I think you're being hasty.' Claudio regarded her calmly. 'Just reflect for a moment and I'm sure you'll realise that it's in your interests as much as it's in mine. Neither of us wants me to have to hang around here. So the sooner your mother and Dino get back, the happier we'll both be.'

'But there's no point in your hanging around here! There's nothing for you to prise out of me! I keep telling you I don't know where my mother and Dino are!'

'I know what you keep telling me. But I don't necessarily believe you. So, like it or not,' he concluded with a warning smile, 'I'll be hanging around until your mother and Dino show up.'

A picture of the large leather holdall he'd brought suddenly flashed across Rachel's mind. There were probably enough clothes in there to last him for a couple of weeks. If it came to it, she wondered, would he really stick around that long?

She glanced up at him and saw the intransigent look in his black eyes. Probably, she thought forlornly. What a ghastly prospect. But what he was suggesting was even more ghastly still. Full of resentment, she glared at him. 'You've completely ruined my holiday.'

'Don't despair.' He smiled back at her in a display of mock-sympathy. 'This could all be over very quickly, if you co-operate. I could be out of your hair in no time. And surely that's the outcome you want?'

There was no need to verify that. Rachel scowled back in silence.

'Look. Think about it for moment...'

He sat forward suddenly, swinging his legs to the ground, so that, momentarily startled, Rachel snatched her own legs back. She saw him smile at that lamentably uptight reaction and felt a flair of annoyance at being wrong-footed yet again. Yet who could really blame her? How could she feel anything but unsettled when six-feet plus of prime muscular man, dressed in nothing but a pair of skimpy swimming-trunks, was virtually sitting on top of her now? She just wasn't used to this sort of thing.

He continued, 'Think about it. If we set the ball rolling, in a couple of days your ordeal could be over. Word travels fast around here. I guarantee it. We'd only have to be seen in public once or twice and the jungle telegraph would soon be beating the news back to Capri.'

That made it sound almost tempting. 'But,' Rachel pointed out, 'How could the news get back to my mother when nobody knows precisely where she is?'

'Ah, that's where you're wrong. One person will know. Her friend Signora Rossi will know for sure...'

'Then why don't you just go to this Signora Rossi and ask her? Surely that's the obvious thing to do?'

'Signora Rossi wouldn't speak to me, and anyway——'

'I'll go, then!' Suddenly, Rachel was smiling. Here was a way out, after all! 'Tell me where she lives. I'll go and ask her for you.'

Claudio smiled back at her. 'Don't worry, I'd already have sent you...' As her eyes flickered with annoyance at that, he added, 'Except for one thing... She and her husband are touring Spain at the moment.'

'Spain?' Rachel's smile was slipping from her face. She might have known the solution wouldn't be that simple. 'In that case,' she added, her tone grown mournful, 'she wouldn't get to know about me and you until she got back.' She glared at him accusingly. 'So much for your claim that it would only take a couple of days!'

'It will.' Before she could protest again, he silenced her with a wave of his hand. 'You see, Signora Rossi is one of these people who likes to keep in touch with what's going on. Even while she's on holiday—and I was told this once by your mother—she's on the phone every day to her friends and neighbours in Florence just to make sure she's not missing anything.'

He narrowed his eyes at Rachel. 'So, you see,' he told her, 'the news about you and me will reach Signora Rossi almost immediately, and then, for sure, she'll be straight on the phone to your mother.'

'I see.' Rachel regarded him with very mixed feelings. He was tricky all right. He'd worked this whole thing out in detail. But if what he was saying was true, then his plan ought to work.

'You really think it would only take a couple of days?' she demanded doubtfully. There was no way she would even consider co-operating if it was going to take longer.

'I can more or less guarantee it.' He smiled. 'Your ordeal would be brief.'

So, this was beginning, after all, to sound like a proposition worth considering. But first there were certain points that needed clarification.

Rachel sat back and fixed him with shrewd hazel eyes. 'And what precisely,' she wanted to know, 'would my ordeal consist of?'

'Nothing too terrible. A couple of romantic dinners. A trip to the theatre or a party to ensure maximum exposure.' He eyed her. 'Surely you know as well as I do what two people who are having a mad, passionate affair get up to?'

'No, I'm afraid I don't. That may be your area of expertise, but I'm afraid it definitely isn't mine.'

Rachel said it without thinking and immediately wished she hadn't, as she realised how revealing it had been.

Claudio was regarding her with interest, just as she'd anticipated. 'What's the matter? Haven't you ever had a mad, passionate affair?'

Rachel thinned her lips at him. No, I haven't, she thought. She and Mark had been quite close and they'd had their tender moments, but they'd never been lovers, passionate or otherwise. In fact, she'd never really thought of Mark in that way at all—as a possible sexual partner and lover. She'd been fond of him, but there'd never been any special spark between them, which was why his proposal of marriage had come as such a total shock to her. And the relationships she'd had before Mark had been equally sexually innocent.

Out loud she retorted, 'Is that any business of yours?'

'Maybe it is.' There was a touch of amusement in his eyes. 'If this is all so new to you, maybe you'll require some tutoring.'

'Hah! That'll be the day!' Rachel sat back firmly in her seat, but managed to resist the impulse to fold her arms across her chest. 'I don't think any tutoring will be required, thank you very much!'

As she said it she was thinking of that kiss he'd inflicted on her. Now's my chance, she told herself, to warn him against any repetitions. But either she hesitated or he was too quick for her for suddenly he was asking curiously, 'I take it this means you haven't got a boyfriend?'

Rachel hesitated for only a second. 'Well, you take it wrong,' she retorted. 'I have got a boyfriend, as it happens.'

It was a lie, of course. She'd had no boyfriend since last week when her relationship with Mark had come to its unexpected and sad end. But, though she hated to tell lies, that one had been necessary. If he believed she had a boyfriend, Claudio might keep his distance.

He was watching her closely. 'That's a surprise,' he said.

'And why should it be a surprise? Having a boyfriend's fairly normal.'

'Very normal indeed.' Claudio smiled in agreement. 'Maybe I'm simply surprised that he isn't over here with you. That strikes me as a little less normal.' He paused and let his gaze flicker over her for a moment, a look that was openly appreciative and as intimate as a caress. 'If you were *my* girlfriend, I wouldn't let you out of my sight for a moment. And I certainly wouldn't allow you to go off on holiday by yourself.'

'Then I'm glad I'm not your girlfriend.' Rachel flicked a look back at him. 'I could never put up with possessiveness like that.'

But, even though she meant it, she was aware that her skin was tingling at the unashamedly sensuous way he was still looking at her. And she found herself thinking, What on earth's got into me? For no man before had ever made her tingle like this.

But Claudio was waiting for her answer. She pulled herself together. 'Mark couldn't come,' she told him, 'because he's teaching summer school for most of the holiday.'

At least the bones of that were true. Mark was indeed teaching summer school.

'So, he's a teacher like you?'

'Yes, he is, and a very good one.'

'And obviously an exceptionally dedicated one, too, since he prefers to teach summer school rather than come to Italy with you.' As he made this observation, Claudio smiled a caustic smile that revealed he wasn't terribly impressed with this relationship.

Rachel felt a flicker of irritation. Trust him to be demeaning! 'He had other commitments, that's all,' she pointed out sharply, reflecting that in the past that had often been the case, that they'd spent holidays apart because one of them was busy. 'Besides,' she added pointedly, 'we don't have the sort of relationship where we feel the need to live in each other's pocket.'

'Why? Don't you enjoy each other's company?'

'Of course we enjoy each other's company. What a silly thing to say. We wouldn't be involved with each other if we didn't!'

But they were no longer involved. What they'd had hadn't been enough. At least, not for Rachel, though Mark had apparently been prepared to settle for it, even though Rachel had always made it quite plain how she felt. No, when it came to a lifetime commitment, Rachel wanted a great deal more than the jog-along relationship that she and Mark had shared. As she'd said, she'd enjoyed his company, but she'd never been excited by it. She'd never felt, even for one moment, that she couldn't live without him. And before she ever agreed to marry someone, she knew she would have to feel like that.

But now she was aware that Claudio was speaking again.

'Well,' he was saying, 'that's good news for us. It's most convenient that you and Mark have such a free and easy relationship. It means that you and I can really go to town and put everything we've got into our little pretend affair.'

'Not so fast.' Rachel glanced across at him sharply. 'I haven't actually agreed to anything yet.'

'Haven't you? I thought you had.'

'Well, I haven't,' Rachel insisted. 'I'm still thinking it over.' She sat back and narrowed her eyes at him. 'For there is another alternative, you know. I could simply move out of the villa and find myself a *pensione*. I don't have to subject myself to your company at all.'

'You wouldn't get away from me that easily.'

'You mean you'd follow me?'

'As the tail follows the dog. I'd make your life a misery, until you finally begged your mother to come hurrying back to San Cappano.'

'But I don't know where my mother is!' Rachel sighed with frustration. She was beginning to feel as though she was going round in circles. And every time she came round again there was Claudio right in front of her. She just couldn't get away from him, however hard she tried!

Besides, her threat to move into a *pensione* had been an idle one. She couldn't afford to move into a *pensione*. The only alternative would be to go home.

Her heart sank at the thought. She didn't want to go home yet. What she wanted was to stay on here and have a nice relaxing time. A nice relaxing time *on her own*!

And suddenly she was so angry she jumped up from her seat, stuffing her hands into the pockets of her Bermudas.

'I'm going for a walk,' she announced. 'Please don't follow me. I need some time on my own to think.'

'Take all the time you need.' Claudio stretched back comfortably on his sunbed. 'After all, I'm not planning on going anywhere.'

Rachel stomped off across the garden. How did I ever get into this? All I was after was a few weeks of peace and quiet, and instead I find myself up to my eyes in this mess! Maybe I ought to go home after all! she was thinking.

At the edge of the garden she climbed on to the wall and sat gazing out at the endless vista of vineyards and olive groves that surrounded the villa. But how could she leave all this when she'd only just arrived? When she hadn't even had a chance to visit Florence yet and see all the art treasures she'd so been looking forward to seeing? It would be such a waste. She would never forgive herself.

No, she was being chicken, she told herself, even to think of leaving. She'd come for three weeks and that was precisely how long she'd stay.

For surely there wasn't really anything to worry about? Surely she could manage to handle Claudio? It was clear he was no saint, but it was equally clear, she was now convinced, that he was not the dangerous sex maniac her mother had painted him. And she wouldn't have to endure him for long. Only for a couple of days.

Then she'd be free of him, she thought, smiling. Free to enjoy the rest of her holiday. Surely a couple of days was a very small sacrifice?

Her mind made up, Rachel headed back to the poolside. But when she reached the sunbed where Claudio had been lying he was no longer there. Damn! she thought. He's done this on purpose. Now I have to go and search for him!

Fortunately, she didn't have to search far. He was in the sitting-room, perched on the arm of the sofa, speaking into the phone.

Rachel stood in the doorway and watched him. He must have left the pool right after her, for he was properly dressed now, in a pair of blue trousers and a plain white T-shirt, his dark hair wet, presumably from the shower. And though he'd made no sign of having noticed her arrival she assumed he almost certainly had. She remembered all too well how he'd tricked her earlier.

So she just leaned against the door-frame and watched him quite openly. After all, it wasn't as though she could be accused of eavesdropping. She couldn't understand a word he was saying!

Although that wasn't quite true. She'd picked up a few 'cara's and a couple of 'amore's. It seemed pretty evident that he was speaking to a woman.

At last, he laid down the phone and turned to look at her, confirming her theory that he'd known all along she was there. She felt rather pleased with herself. She was starting to suss him out.

'So,' he said, 'you're back from your walk. Did you manage to come to any decisions?'

Rachel took a deep breath. He had stood up from the chair-arm and suddenly he looked very dark and tall and dangerous. She had a sudden last-minute panic. Was what she was about to do wise?

But she chastised herself silently. Don't be a wimp, Rachel, she told herself. 'Yes, I have,' she told him, keeping him in suspense for a moment, for she could see that he was curious to discover what she'd decided.

He stepped towards her. 'And?' he enquired.

Rachel fixed his face for a moment with serious hazel eyes. 'I've decided,' she said slowly, 'to go along with you for a couple of days. We can try this little charade of yours and see if it works.'

'Good.' Claudio nodded. 'Then I suggest we start. We can have dinner in Florence at a favourite restaurant of mine.'

Rachel was a little taken aback at the way she was being plunged in straight away. 'Couldn't we start tomorrow?' she protested a little lamely.

'I thought you wanted this over quickly?'

'I do, but——'

'Then we'll start tonight. The sooner we start, the sooner it'll all be over. Besides,' he added with a hint of a smile, 'I've just cancelled the date I had fixed for tonight.'

As her eyebrows rose, he continued, 'I suggest we leave about eight, but we can meet down here about half-seven and have a drink together to get us in the mood.' He looked her up and down. 'Wear something nice,' he instructed. Then he swept past her. 'I'm going upstairs to finish unpacking.'

And with that he was gone. Rachel stared after him, blinking. 'Wear something nice'! Who did he think he was? And what was that cute remark about getting in the mood? She might be prepared to go through the motions of this stupid charade, but she certainly had no intention of getting in the mood!

But the thing that irked her most was the way he'd taken it for granted that she would agree to play this silly game with him. Before she'd even given him her answer, he'd actually had the arrogance to go ahead and cancel his date!

* * *

It was about six-thirty, while Rachel was in her room
getting ready to have a shower and wash her hair for
the evening, that she heard a familiar roar coming
from the driveway down below. Wrapping her robe
around her, she darted to the window and was just in
time to catch a glimpse of Claudio, sitting astride the
big black and silver motorbike, disappearing out
through the gate.

That was interesting, she reflected. Perhaps he had
changed his mind and decided to call off their dinner
date without telling her.

It was the height of rudeness, of course, but she
couldn't say she was sorry. An evening on her own
was bound to be more pleasant than an evening with
Claudio.

Still, she went ahead and had her shower and
washed her hair, and it was as she was standing by
the wardrobe wondering whether she should bother
getting dressed that she heard footsteps coming along
the corridor.

He's back, she thought with a sinking feeling.

An instant later, to confirm that, he tapped on her
door in passing. 'I hope you're nearly ready? It's
twenty past seven. I'll expect to see you downstairs
in about ten minutes.' An instant later she heard his
bedroom door close with a click.

Damned martinet. Rachel pointedly didn't answer.
So, this was the way he planned the evening to go,
was it—with him snapping his fingers and her mutely
obeying? She glowered into the wardrobe. Well, he
was wrong if he thought that. Just because she'd

agreed to go along with this little plot of his, it didn't mean she was going to do everything he said!

She scowled at the row of hangers, trying to decide what to wear. 'Wear something nice,' he'd said in that imperious way he had—which almost tempted her to pick out an old pair of shorts and a T-shirt! But that would be silly. This would be her first outing in Florence and she wanted to wear something nice in celebration—though it irked her that he'd assume she was doing it for him.

So let him delude himself! That was his problem. Rachel drew out a long-skirted dress in deep purple that she knew looked quite stunning with her red hair and pale skin. She would wear it with the purple espadrilles she'd bought in London and her favourite dangly green and purple earrings.

Ten minutes later she was ready, but she deliberately wasted a few more minutes tidying up the bathroom and checking her hair. Normally she was punctual, but she'd be utterly damned if she was going to arrive downstairs on the stroke of seven-thirty for him!

It was twenty-four minutes to eight when she eventually sauntered into the drawing-room.

'Sorry if I kept you waiting——' she began. But then she came to an abrupt halt, entirely forgetting what she'd planned to say next, as she caught sight of Claudio standing by the stereo near the window, apparently examining her mother and Dino's collection of CDs. It was quite shocking but the sight of him had made her breath catch in her throat.

He was dressed in a superbly cut off-white suit with a light blue shirt open at the neck and she had never seen a man look more delicious in her life.

In the soft evening light the cool, subtle colours made a wonderful contrast to the deep tan of his skin and the rich, glossy blackness of his swept-back hair. And the immaculate cut of the suit enhanced to perfection the lean, masculine lines of his perfectly honed body—the broad shoulders, the narrow hips, the hard length of his legs.

And in some extraordinary way he managed to look even more sexually dangerous than he had earlier when he'd been wearing only an insubstantial pair of swimming-trunks. Behind the sleek, sophisticated exterior one could sense the vibrant potency, and it was all the more vivid for being hidden.

He had turned to look at her and evidently his thoughts about her were similar.

'A red-haired Aida,' he smiled, 'all dressed in imperial purple.' As he spoke, he returned to its place on the shelf behind him the CD of Verdi's opera that he had been studying. 'Well, if she looked like you, I can see why Radames chose to die rather than lose her.'

Rachel was not too familiar with the plot of *Aida*. 'If you say so,' she said, trying not to look impressed, though she had found the compliment rather appealing.

It was the novelty of it, she told herself. That was what had appealed to her. For no one had ever compared her to an operatic heroine before. But at the same time, she reminded herself, she would be mad to take it seriously. This was Claudio del'Angelo, the arch-seducer, she was dealing with. He probably handed out these colourful compliments to every woman he took to dinner.

'Would you like a glass of wine before we go? As you can see, I've already helped myself to one.' He took a mouthful from the long-stemmed glass in his hand, and added with a wicked smile, 'Just to get you in the mood.'

'No, thanks. If you don't mind, I'll skip that part.'

Rachel had expected him to chastise her for arriving downstairs late. She felt slightly wrong-footed that he had failed to do so. And that was partly why she refused his offer of a drink. Out of sheer contrariness. Just to cross him. And partly also to make it clear that his exhortations to get in the mood were destined to fall on determinedly deaf ears.

But her contrariness simply amused him. 'OK,' he said, smiling. He drained his glass and laid it down on a nearby table. Then he raised his eyes to hers again. 'Since you're ready, let's go. Besides,' he added, 'I have a much more foolproof idea for getting you in the mood.'

'Really?' You're fooling yourself, Rachel's tone told him plainly. She cast him a cool, sceptical, hazel-eyed look and observed in a tone that expressed the very opposite, 'I can't wait to find out what on earth that could be.'

'Then follow me.' Claudio proceeded to lead her out into the hallway. Next moment they were stepping out on to the gravel driveway.

And that was when Rachel got her first big surprise of the evening. For parked where she had expected his motorbike to be was a low-slung silver Maserati.

Claudio laughed at the look of surprise on her face. 'You didn't really expect me to take you out to dinner on the back of a motorbike?' He was reaching down to pull open the passenger door for her. As she slid past him into the cool, leather-scented interior, he caught her eye and winked. 'Only the very best for my red-haired Aida.'

So that was where he'd gone off to earlier, when she'd wondered if he'd run out on her, Rachel reflected as he came round to slide in behind the wheel. He'd gone home to exchange the motorbike for the Maserati. And suddenly she found herself wondering curiously where he lived and what his house was like— and, just by the way, how many other forms of transport he had at his disposal! Though she switched off these thoughts immediately. She wished to know nothing about him!

'So, where are you taking me?'

Rachel glanced across at him as with a growl the powerful car set off down the road. She rather hoped that wherever it was it wasn't any great distance, for she didn't much care for being cooped up in this little car with him. Every time he changed gear she was horribly aware of his nearness and she was far too conscious of the hard, muscular thighs that seemed only inches away from her own. It was an effort to keep her gaze firmly through the windscreen.

'I'm taking you to one of my favourite restaurants. But first I have a special little treat in store.'

This was the special little treat that was supposed to 'get her in the mood'. Rachel made a face to herself and pointedly declined to ask him to elaborate. He would discover soon enough that he was wasting his time.

It was only about fifteen minutes before they were approaching the city.

'That's the Boboli Gardens,' Claudio told her as they passed what looked like an enormous park. 'You must be sure to visit them some time while you're here.'

'I intend to.' The gardens were one of the many things on her list, which she intended making a start on first thing tomorrow.

'And this is the Viale di Poggio Imperiale.' Suddenly they were swinging up a wide, winding avenue, illuminated on either side by tall, elegant lamp posts. And then, a few minutes later, as they swung into a huge open piazza, he announced, 'And this is the Piazzale Michelangelo.'

Rachel gasped as he brought the car to a halt in the middle of the square, where half a dozen or so other cars were already parked. And, forgetting for a moment to be uncooperative and unimpressed, she leaned forward, her eyes widening in wonder as she saw the famous statue that dominated the piazzale from its high central plinth.

'Then that,' she gasped, 'must be Michelangelo's David!'

'You're right, it is.' Claudio glanced across at her. 'Shall we get out for a moment and admire the view?'

Rachel was already reaching impatiently for the door-handle. Try and stop me! she felt like saying.

And the view, it turned out, was every bit as spectacular as promised in all the guidebooks she'd been reading.

The piazzale was set high up in the hills south-east of the city, a broad iron balustrade running the length of its city-facing perimeter. And as Rachel stepped towards the balustrade, where several small groups of people were gathered, and leaned against it, just as they were doing, she could see the entire city spread out below her, all rich, soft ochres and rosy terra-cottas, with the silver thread of the River Arno running in between.

She let out a gasp of wonder. 'I've never seen anything so beautiful!'

Claudio had come to stand beside her. 'That's the Duomo,' he told her, pointing to the magnificent cathedral that dominated the vista. 'And just in front, that tall building, that's the Palazzo Vecchio. And that white church there, that's Santa Croce.'

'It's incredible!' Rachel was aware that he'd slipped one arm round her waist. She wondered fleetingly if she ought to protest, but somehow it didn't seem to matter.

'And that,' she exclaimed, pointing, 'must be the Ponte Vecchio!' She gazed at the famous bridge, built in the fourteenth century, with its goldsmiths and precious jewellery shops. 'This is wonderful. I can hardly believe it!'

'I'm glad you like it.'

'Like it? I think it's fabulous.' Rachel cast a quick glance round at the statue of David. 'Lucky chap. He has one of the most spectacular views in the world.'

The arm around her waist had tightened a little. Claudio was standing very close now, his warmth embracing her. 'You realise, of course, that that's not the original David. It's only a copy. The original's in the Accademia.'

Rachel had read that in her guidebook. She nodded. 'Yes, I know, and I intend to go and see the original while I'm here.' Then she sighed as she turned back to the amazing vista below her. 'There's so much to see. I'll never be able to pack it into three weeks!'

'That's for sure. I haven't finished discovering Florence myself yet.' Claudio smiled. 'And I've lived here all my life.'

'Then what hope is there for me?'

Rachel smiled a light smile and turned to look at him as she said it. But the oddest sensation went through her as she met his eyes—a rush of excitement and happiness and heady attraction, so vivid and intense it made her heart crack. Just for an instant, she felt utterly stunned.

Then she tore her gaze away. I'm crazy, she told herself. I'm letting the magic of this city go to my head.

Abruptly, oddly panic-stricken, she started to turn away, trying as she did so to disentangle his arm from her waist. She'd been out of her mind to let him hold her like that.

But the arm around her waist remained firmly where it was. 'Who knows who might be watching us?'

Claudio leaned towards her, as though whispering some romantic endearment in her ear. 'Remember, we're playing the part of lovers.'

'But surely there's no one here who knows my mother or Dino?'

'There could well be. This is a favourite spot for Florentines. It's not just the tourists who come up here to enjoy the view.' To Rachel's horror, he bent down suddenly to kiss her, his lips brushing lingeringly, sensuously, over hers. 'So it would be foolish to waste a perfect opportunity to get this rumour going.'

As he kissed her again, Rachel froze and just stood there—a bit like that first time when he'd kissed her outside the villa. But though she felt stiff and paralysed and quite unable to react, she was aware that it was not a resisting stiffness. She simply felt helpless, quite overcome by the torrent of emotions and sensations flooding through her.

Her mind had gone blank. All at once, she felt quite breathless. And her heart felt as though it might jump out of her chest. But what was strangest of all, and quite beyond fighting, was the realisation that she had never enjoyed anything half so much in her life!

Then all too soon, it seemed, Claudio was taking her by the hand. 'Come on. Let's go. Our table's waiting.'

He led her across the piazzale to the waiting Maserati, his fingers cool as they laced with hers. And though Rachel was trying very hard to get a grip on reality, she was painfully aware that she was doing a pretty hopeless job.

For, through her paralysis, she was filled with a giddy sense of magic, as though a battery of coloured lights were flashing on and off in her head. And though she was struggling with all her strength to make contact with the ground, the truth was she was really floating about six feet in the air.

CHAPTER FOUR

RACHEL had recovered her senses by the time they reached the restaurant.

On the short journey in the car she'd given herself a good talking-to. She was treading on dangerous ground. One thing she must not do was in any way confuse the very real magic of Florence with the utterly and totally false magic of Claudio.

Not that she was susceptible to Claudio's magic, false or otherwise, anyway. All that had happened back at the piazzale was that he had caught her unawares.

The restaurant he took her to was near the Piazza delila Signoria, down a narrow side-street in the direction of the river. 'It's a very popular place,' he told her, motioning her to enter in front of him. 'Somebody's bound to see us here.'

'Let's hope so.' As Rachel stepped inside, she threw him a grim look. 'And let's hope the news gets back to Capri really fast.'

'In that case, try to do a little better than you did up in the piazzale.' Claudio spoke quickly to the waiter, then turned back to Rachel again. 'As a demonstration of raw passion that left a great deal to be desired. If you act like that,' he added as the waiter led them to their table, 'people will think I'm having dinner with my sister, not my girlfriend.'

Arrogant pig! Did he expect her to jump all over him? Rachel glared vindictively at the back of his head as the waiter led them through the throng of noisy tables. Though he was quite right, of course, she acknowledged. She'd seemed to turn to wood. In fact, all in all, she'd acted most strangely!

The restaurant was much bigger than it had looked from the street and every table appeared to be taken. But there was one free, right at the back, half hidden in a corner, and that was where the waiter was leading them now. As he handed them their menus and silently departed, Rachel threw Claudio a caustic look.

'Well,' she observed, 'this isn't very clever. You might have had the foresight to book a more visible table. Nobody's going to see us here.'

To her annoyance in response Claudio smiled a smug smile. 'Obviously you're not familiar with one of the basic rules of human nature. The more one tries to hide and remain anonymous, the more attention one inevitably draws to oneself.' He smiled again at her annoyed look and went on to assure her, 'Right now, every single person in this entire restaurant is wondering who the couple are who require so much privacy. Believe me, every eye in the place is on us.'

He leaned forward suddenly, reached for her hand across the table and raised it unhurriedly to his lips. 'And now,' he added, smiling wickedly, 'they're even more curious than ever.'

Rachel had felt herself stiffen the minute his hand had touched hers. Her instinctive reaction had been to jerk it away. And he had expected that. She had felt his grip tighten. As his lips lightly grazed the back of her hand, all at once her fingers were caught in a vice.

'Try to look at though you're enjoying it,' he gritted between his teeth.

'How can I? You're hurting me!' But she forced a smile all the same. Though it was a relief when he finally released her fingers. She had to stop herself from shaking them to get the circulation going again!

Claudio was shaking his head at her. 'I can see this is going to be an uphill struggle. You really haven't a clue what passion's about.'

'Yes, I do. I just don't happen to feel any for you. Especially when you're squeezing all the blood out of my fingers!'

Privately, though, she was reflecting that he was right. Passion had never been a noticeable ingredient in her life. She found herself glancing at Claudio and reflecting that it would be in his. Something stirred inside her, something almost wistful, and she was rather glad to see the waiter arriving to take their orders.

'What I feel like is a nice big plate of pasta.' Claudio glanced across the table at Rachel with a warm smile. 'Have you decided yet, *cara*?' he asked.

'*Cara*'. That was a nice touch. Rachel forced a smile back at him, though she was aware that all this play-acting came less easily to her.

She pulled a face and scanned the menu, which up until now she'd barely glanced at. 'I'm not really sure. What do you suggest?'

And though she'd fully intended to drop a casual 'darling' in there somewhere, when it actually came to it, the endearment stuck in her throat. Come on, Rachel, she thought crossly. You're going to blow this if you're not careful. The way he's acting, no one's going to think for one minute that you're his sister, but what they will think, if they look at you, is that you're giving him the brush-off!

'Try the *penne alla zingara*. That's what I'm going to have.' Claudio's eyes, as he answered her question, seemed to embrace her across the table. He really was an excellent performer.

'OK.' The look in Rachel's eyes was pathetically unembracing, and she wasn't the least bit surprised when Claudio told the waiter, 'And a large carafe of your best white wine at once, please.' He was probably hoping, as she was, that a couple of glasses of wine might loosen her up!

The wine was brought and two generous glassfuls poured. But, before she could take a swig, Claudio leaned across the table and, holding out his glass to her, proposed a romantic toast.

'To us,' he purred, his eyes pouring over her. 'May we always be as much in love as we are tonight.'

Very funny. Rachel refrained from pulling a face and did her best to respond appropriately. Then she took a large mouthful. There, that ought to help.

'I think it would be a good idea if we got to know a bit about each other.' Claudio had sat back slightly in his seat and was watching her across the table. 'You know, just a few details about each other's personal life. The sort of little titbits one exchanges across the pillow after a particularly satisfying session of lovemaking.'

There'd been no need to add that last bit. He'd only done it to make her blush. And, to Rachel's annoyance, that was what she duly did as her stomach tightened disgracefully inside her.

Claudio smiled. 'Just in case we find ourselves in company,' he added. 'We don't want to appear like total strangers.'

'OK. What do you want to know?' At least it looked, Rachel thought, as though the conversation was about to become a little more safe and neutral. Though, knowing Claudio, she wasn't banking on that. He could turn any topic into a minefield.

He took a mouthful of his wine. 'Tell me about where you live. Tell me about your schoolteaching. What do you teach, for example?'

'I teach English at a secondary school in Bristol. That's a city in the south-west of England where I've lived all my life. The kids I teach are fourteen- and fifteen-year-olds, for the most part.'

'And do you enjoy it?'

'I enjoy it very much. Ever since I was a kid I always wanted to be a teacher.'

'Your father was a teacher, if I'm not mistaken?'

'He taught science. Physics. He was a very clever man. But I hardly knew him. He died when I was eight.'

'That must have been hard—I mean growing up without a father.'

Rachel was surprised to see a look of real sympathy in his eyes. Was he capable, after all, of real human feeling? She found that possibility a little disconcerting.

She said, 'I suppose, really, it was hardest on my mother. She had three daughters to bring up alone on very little money. It can't have been much fun for her.'

Claudio made no comment, but the sympathy in his eyes had vanished at that innocent reference to her mother. Just for a moment there was a flash of anger in their depths. His antipathy towards Dino and her mother obviously went very deep.

But why? Rachel wondered. What could possibly be at the root of it? Did Dino really owe him a large sum of money, as he'd claimed? Rachel found it hard to believe—especially knowing her mother. For her mother had always been utterly scrupulous in money matters. Even in the bad old days, when she'd scarcely had two pennies, she'd always paid her bills on the dot.

Just for a moment, as the waiter brought their *penne alla zingara*, Rachel felt tempted to pursue the subject. But then she thought better of it. This was neither the time nor the place. So, as he handed her the grated Parmesan, she asked him instead, 'Did you always want to be an architect?'

'Actually, no.' Claudio shook his head. 'You won't believe this, but there was a time when I wanted to become a professional footballer. I even auditioned for Fiorentina, the local club.'

He smiled. 'My parents were absolutely horrified. They were rather hoping I'd become a lawyer, like my

father and my brother and my sister. The law's a bit
of a tradition in our family.

'Anyway, they were greatly relieved when the club
told me I was too young and that I ought to come
back for another audition the following year. Though
I never went back for that second audition, for by
then I'd decided I wanted to become an architect. My
parents were so relieved that I'd gone off the idea of
being a footballer, they didn't even bother trying to
persuade me to take up law. They just said, "Thank
heavens. Go ahead and be an architect."'

He laughed as he finished his story and Rachel
laughed with him, watching him with sudden pleasure
across the table. And as she did so it struck her how
easily he laughed and how easily that smile of his came
to his lips. It was really rather refreshing. In spite of
all his bad points, he didn't seem to take himself too
seriously. It was a side to him, she decided, that she
very much liked.

But at that very moment they were suddenly being
borne down on by a voluptuous, dark-haired female
in a tight-fitting red dress.

'Claudio! I thought that was you, hiding there in
the corner!' Before Claudio even had a chance to rise
to his feet to greet her, the young woman was leaning
over him to deliver a kiss on each cheek.

Rachel found herself watching the scene with acute
interest—and also with a degree of mild alarm. For
the way she was bending forward, the young woman's
copious *décolletage* looked in imminent danger of
sliding into Claudio's *penne alla zingara*. Golly,
Rachel thought, that would make a bit of a mess!

'No, don't get up.' As she at last detached her cheek from Claudio's, the young woman laid a restraining arm on his shoulder. 'Instead, why don't you introduce me to your delightful companion?' She turned to Rachel with a smile that could have skinned tomatoes. 'We're all just dying to know who she is.'

Claudio instantly went into action.

'This is Rachel.' His tongue curled lovingly round the syllables of her name, making it sound less like an introduction and more like a declaration of love. He leaned across the table and took Rachel's hand in his. 'Rachel, *amore*, this is Kirsten.'

Wow, Rachel thought, glancing at him, that was good!

Then she turned to the young woman with the precarious *décolletage* whose hand, she noticed, was still attached to Claudio's shoulder. And, as something sparked inside her, suddenly she was acting, too.

'Hello, Kirsten,' she purred. 'How lovely to meet a friend of Claudio's.' And as she said his name she glanced quickly in his direction and almost managed to sound as utterly smitten as he had.

Well, she thought with pride, that was pretty good too!

'You're English, I see. Are you here on holiday?'

Kirsten was still having difficulty controlling the daggers in her eyes. She looked very much as though she was privately hoping that Rachel might announce she was due to leave tomorrow.

Rachel smiled and glanced again across the table at Claudio, then laid her cheek against his fingers which were entwined lovingly with hers. 'I originally came here on holiday,' she cooed, 'but who knows how long I'll be staying now? Now,' she added dreamily, 'that I've met Claudio.'

'Don't even think of leaving. I'd only come after you.' Claudio's tone was a pained and loving entreaty. He glanced at Kirsten. 'Who could blame me? Isn't she gorgeous?'

Rachel thought for a moment that Kirsten was about to turn green. She felt quite shocked at how little that prospect displeased her. But then Claudio said, 'Mind you, Kirsten, I must say you're looking pretty gorgeous yourself tonight. I've always said that red was your colour.'

Instantly, Kirsten brightened. 'Why, thank you, Claudio! How very gallant of you to say so.'

And as she glanced at Rachel, Rachel had to fight quite hard to stop her dreamy smile from faltering just a bit. There'd been no need for him to say that, she thought crossly. Tonight he was supposed to have eyes only for her!

Not that I really care, of course, she reminded herself sharply as, redressing the balance, Claudio bent to kiss her fingertips. I just don't want him to wreck this little show we're putting on.

But no damage had been done. Clearly feeling a bit of a gooseberry, Kirsten was reluctantly taking her leave of them.

'I'd better be getting back. My friends are waiting for me.' She gestured vaguely towards a crowded table at the back. 'I'll see you around, Claudio,' she added with a wink.

As she disappeared off, Claudio turned to Rachel. 'I would say that deserved an Oscar,' he told her, smiling. 'Or, at the very least, another glass of wine.' With his free hand he proceeded to fill up her wine glass. 'So,' he observed, 'you can do it when you try.'

'Of course I can. What made you think I couldn't?' Though the truth was, Rachel reflected, she hadn't really had to try much. Her performance, to her own surprise, had come quite naturally. It hadn't required any effort at all.

Perhaps it had been the wine. She smiled and took another mouthful. She'd thoroughly enjoyed that little charade.

But there was one question she had to ask. 'Kirsten wasn't, by any chance, the date you cancelled in order to come here with me?'

'No, she wasn't.' Claudio shook his head. 'Kirsten and I had nothing planned for tonight.'

'Nothing planned for tonight'. For some reason his response irked her. A little stiffly, Rachel found herself saying. 'So, she's one of your girlfriends, then?'

'One of the legion of girlfriends your mother likes to talk about?' Claudio smiled and shrugged, but did not deny it. 'Kirsten and I have been known to spend time together now and then.'

That had been obvious. Rachel found herself remembering the proprietorial way Kirsten had laid her hand on Claudio's shoulder and then, even more irritatingly, left it there. And then there had been that final, irritating wink. What exactly had been the secret message behind that wink?

Then she drew herself up short. What was going on with her? This was only a *pretend* romance she was having with Claudio! She didn't give a damn what was going on between him and Kirsten! Was she out of her mind reacting like this?

She hurriedly pulled herself together as Claudio told her, nodding towards the table that Kirsten had disappeared off to, 'These friends Kirsten's with . . . one of them's a renowned gossip. Which is good news for us.' He smiled across at her. 'Half the restaurant by now probably knows your name and where you come from, and with any luck, by tomorrow, so will half of Florence.

'Which means that word will soon be winging its way down the telephone wires to Signora Rossi—and from Signora Rossi to your mother in Capri.'

Well, if that wasn't the case, Rachel reflected a couple of hours later, after they'd had their coffee and it was time to leave, it wouldn't be for any lack of effort on their part. They'd put on a wonderful performance throughout the rest of the meal, laughing in that way that lovers laughed together, gazing into each other's eyes and holding hands across the table. It had been an admirable effort. They'd really pulled out all the stops.

Though as they left the restaurant and made their way back to the car Rachel wondered if Claudio wasn't taking things a little too far when he suddenly caught hold of her and kissed her right there in the street.

Still, she didn't protest. Maybe someone was watching them. Instead, merely being co-operative, she curled her arms round his neck and offered her lips to him with a sigh of feigned ecstasy. I'm doing this in the interests of freedom, she told herself as she kissed him back and ran her fingers through his hair, which, she reflected, was as soft and as slippery as silk. And it was nothing but pretence when she gasped and shivered as he deepened his kiss and pressed hard against her. This was just like two actors making love on a film set. The passion seemed real—even on her part—but it was actually no more real than a bunch of plastic grapes.

All the same, when he finally released her a few minutes later, Rachel was aware of a decided increase in her heart-rate. She shook back her hair. It was only very slight. No more than if she'd just done a fifty-yard sprint. And it was easily explained. It had been a fairly strenuous kiss. One thing she was sure of was that her reaction wasn't emotional.

She glanced around her with a half-smile. 'Did you see someone you knew? Was someone watching us?' she asked him.

Claudio smiled and quite unhurriedly reached out one hand to smooth back a curl that had fallen over her forehead. 'No, as a matter of fact, there wasn't. I just did it because I felt like it. And I rather enjoyed it,' he told her. 'Didn't you?'

Rachel glared at him, outraged. 'What do you mean, you just felt like it? That wasn't the deal! You had no business doing that! And no,' she added hastily, fixing him with a cool look, 'as it happens I didn't enjoy it in the least!'

They had reached the car. Claudio pulled open the passenger door. 'That's a pity,' he observed, smiling down at her wickedly. 'Still, never mind. I reckon I enjoyed it enough for both of us.'

He thought he was so smart, but Rachel was damned if she'd let him get away with it. As he climbed in beside her and they headed south to San Cappano, she continued to make her feelings heard.

'If you're going to take liberties like that,' she fumed at him, 'you can forget about any co-operation on my part. So I'm afraid I want your word that nothing like that will ever happen again.'

'My word?' Claudio laughed. 'That sounds very serious.' Then, 'OK,' he agreed, glancing at her. 'It won't happen again.'

They made the journey back to San Cappano in prickly silence. At least, Rachel's side of the silence was prickly. Claudio appeared to be enjoying the music on the car radio, even humming along with bits of it from time to time. He clearly didn't give a damn how furious she was. And one thing was for certain: he was suffering no remorse.

As soon as they arrived at the villa, Rachel jumped out of the car. And she kept her distance as Claudio led the way to the front door. In spite of his promise, she didn't really trust him and there was no way she wanted to be caught out again.

'I hope you were listening to what I was saying in the car,' she told him as he stuck the key in the lock and pushed the door open. Good grief, she was thinking, I've got to spend the whole night here alone with him. What if he takes it into his head to take advantage?

As he turned to smile at her, she was trying to remember if there was a lock on her bedroom door. If there isn't, she told herself, I'll jam a chair under the handle. Or, better still, I'll use the chest of drawers as a barricade. But before Claudio could answer her question suddenly the phone in the hall was ringing.

'I'll get it,' Rachel said instantly, pushing past him. Maybe, she was thinking, it was her mother, in which case she would simply demand that she come back immediately and get her out of this fearful situation. The way things were going, who knew what might happen next?

But, as she picked up the receiver, it was definitely not her mother.

A woman's voice answered her 'Hello' in Italian. And, though Rachel hadn't a clue what she was saying, there was one word she had no difficulty whatsoever in recognising. 'Claudio,' the woman kept saying. '*Voglio parlare con* Claudio.'

With a scowl Rachel held out the receiver towards him. 'It's for you,' she said. 'Some woman wants to speak to you.'

Privately, she reflected, Now I know what that wink meant. Almost certainly the voice on the phone had been Kirsten's.

Well, good luck to her, Rachel told herself as she made her way upstairs to her bedroom. If Kirsten wanted to run after him, that was her stupid business. Though Claudio had a nerve handing out her mother's phone number to all his girlfriends!

Still, who cared? They were all more than welcome to him. Rachel kicked off her shoes and tossed her bag down on the bed. As far as she was concerned, Kirsten and his legion of other girlfriends could fight over the wretched man to their hearts' content. Personally, she wouldn't touch a Lothario like him with a bargepole.

'Are you in there?'

There was a tap on the half-open door. Rachel turned to find Claudio standing watching her.

'I just thought I'd drop by and let you know I'm going out now,' he told her.

Rachel nodded. 'I see.' She did not ask, With Kirsten? After all, after that wink and everything, it scarcely needed asking.

'Have a peaceful night,' Claudio told her. 'I'll see you tomorrow.'

As he closed the door, Rachel stood and listened to his footsteps receding along the corridor and then down the stairs. Then, a moment later, as she was slipping out of her purple dress and hanging it carefully on its hanger, she heard the Maserati roar off into the night.

She stood for a moment and suddenly found herself glancing at the shiny brass lock on the bedroom door. She smiled a wry smile. So there would have been no need, after all, to move all the furniture about as she'd planned.

Then with a sigh she turned away, trying very hard to ignore the tight little knot of tension in her chest which, though it couldn't possibly be disappointment, felt uncomfortably like it.

*   *   *

Next morning, when Rachel went down to the kitchen to get some breakfast, there was a note with a printed card attached waiting for her on the breakfast-table.

'I have to go in to work this morning,' the note advised her, 'but I suggest we have lunch together, just for the sake of appearances. Come to my studio about one o'clock.' It was signed with a large, imposing-looking 'C'.

Well, maybe I will and maybe I won't, Rachel told herself a little grumpily as she read it. Who did he think he was, ordering her about before she'd even had breakfast?

Still, as she switched on the espresso machine, she studied the attached card. 'Claudio del'Angelo, *Architteto*', it announced, with, below it his studio address in Via della Vigna Nuova in Florence. Very interesting, she thought. But maybe I'd rather have lunch alone.

But as she sat down a few minutes later with a cup of *caffelatte* and a brioche, she flicked open her guidebook to study the map inside. Via della Vigna Nuova was close to the centre, near the Arno. So one thing was certain: it wouldn't be difficult to find. She slipped the card inside the guidebook, closed the guidebook and tossed it aside.

We'll see, she decided, deciding nothing. We'll see how I feel when one o'clock arrives.

Rachel dressed sensibly—in a pair of jeans and a lemon top and a pair of comfortable flat sandals for walking—and, straight after breakfast, took a bus into Florence. Then she spent most of the morning wandering round the fabulous Galleria degli Uffizi, marvelling at the breathtaking art treasures on the walls. And though she did her very best to see all she could, after about two and a half hours, like millions of tourists before her, she'd come to the conclusion that it would take a lifetime to see it all properly.

Besides, at least for the time being, she'd reached cultural saturation-point. She'd come back another time and carry on where she'd left off. And in the meantime, she decided, she'd take a stroll round the city.

Leaving the gallery, she crossed the elegant Piazza della Signoria, with its busy pavement cafés and horse-drawn carriages for hire, and headed towards the magnificent cathedral. Then she turned riverwards again to drool at the shoe shops in Via Calzaiuoli and took a leisurely stroll across the Piazza della Repubblica. And for some reason, at that point, she glanced at her watch.

It was a few minutes after one. She felt a clench inside her. Should she go and find a pizzeria somewhere and have lunch by herself, or should she go and find Claudio's studio?

She pulled her map from her bag and studied it for a moment, only to discover that, by some inexplicable coincidence, she was only a short walk away from Via della Vigna Nuova. But still she hesitated. Did she really want to see him? Would it not be more pleasant just to have lunch on her own?

But even as she was debating, almost of their own accord her feet were taking her in the direction of the river. She was still debating when she found herself outside his studio door.

She rang the bell and waited, still feeling uncertain. And when her ring was greeted with only silence, she heaved a small sigh of relief. Obviously he hadn't waited for her. Well, that was just fine. She'd go and find a pizzeria, after all.

But it was just as she was about to walk away that there was a crackle on the entryphone.

'*Chi è?*' demanded a voice she recognised instantly despite the crackles.

She stopped in her tracks and turned round slowly to stare at the polished brass entryphone grille. Then she took a step towards it. It would be rude not to answer.

'It's me,' she said. 'But I can go away if you're busy.'

Instantly there was a buzz and the front door opened. 'Come up. Take the lift. I'm on the top floor.'

Rachel did as she was told and as she stepped out of the lift Claudio was waiting for her by his open studio door. And it was utterly foolish, but her heart clenched at the sight of him and a sensation like caressing fingers went trickling down her spine. She'd seen some beautiful sights this morning, but none more beautiful than him.

What a ridiculous thought! Rachel hurriedly pushed it from her as he smiled at her and told her, 'Welcome. Come on in.'

He was wearing light beige trousers and a pink shirt rolled back to the elbows, and as he led her into his studio it was clear that he had been working. In the middle of the huge room, with its expanse of attic windows that shed a warm, rosy light in every direction, stood a vast architect's desk covered in intricate-looking drawings, with a half-finished cup of coffee in one corner.

Rachel hovered uncertainly. For some reason she felt strange here. This was very much his territory. This was a part of his life she was entering. In here, she sensed, resided the real Claudio del'Angelo, and she wasn't really sure if she wanted to come face to face with him.

'If you're busy,' she said, 'I can easily go.'

'Nonsense. It's been a hectic morning, but I've finished for the moment.' He cast her a look of mild chastisement. 'And what do you mean you can easily go? I invited you, in case you'd forgotten.'

'No, I hadn't forgotten, but maybe lunch isn't necessary. I mean——' Rachel gave a shrug '—we put on a pretty good performance last night.'

Claudio smiled at that, but it was a softer smile than usual. It lacked the usual sharp, cutting edge. His eyes seemed to drift thoughtfully over her face for a moment.

Then he told her, 'Let me show you quickly round the studio, then we'll go and have a nice long, lazy lunch.'

For the next fifteen minutes Rachel listened in fascination as he told her all about the workings of the studio.

'The administrative offices are on the two floors down below,' he explained, 'but this is where all the real work gets done.'

Then as she started asking questions he showed her some of his drawings and explained something about the projects he was working on.

'It's fascinating.' Rachel would happily have stayed there all afternoon. But then she gasped as they suddenly came to an open window with a heart-stopping view over the red roofs of Florence and just a glimpse of the River Arno and the Ponte Santa Trinita.

She leaned against the sill and gazed out with a happy smile. 'So this is where you get all your inspiration from!'

As she spoke, she turned to glance at him, not realising that he'd come to stand behind her. As her heart jolted, she turned back swiftly to look at the view again. Oh, dear, she thought, what's going to happen now?

'I guess it is pretty inspirational, even though by now I'm used to it.'

He seemed to be standing only inches away from her. Rachel fancied she could feel his breath ruffle her hair.

'Can one ever get used to this?'

Rachel had been almost afraid to speak, in case her voice might reveal the sudden chaos inside her. That jolt to her heart as she'd looked into his eyes had shaken her right down to the well-worn soles of her sandals.

Maybe, after all, I shouldn't have come, she was thinking. Suddenly everything seemed to be slipping out of her control.

Claudio seemed quite unaware of her turmoil. His tone was light as he asked her now, 'So you really do like my city, it seems?'

'I think it's wonderful. I went to the Uffizi this morning, then I had a bit of a tour around the centre.'

Rachel was wondering if she had the strength to turn round again and face him. She couldn't continue this conversation indefinitely with her back turned.

She forced herself and swung round, realising as she did so that he wasn't, in fact, standing quite as close as she'd believed—though still close enough to keep her heart hammering against her ribs. 'It really is as lovely as they say,' she muttered.

'I'm glad you like it. I'm rather fond of it myself.' Claudio smiled. 'As I said before, I'm used to it by now—but not to the point where I could ever take it for granted.'

As he stood there before her with the sun on his face, Rachel found herself examining his features in close detail. His eyes were like black velvet, fringed with long, silky lashes. They were wonderful eyes. Eyes to drown in. And that nose. So strong, so aristocratic. And he really did have the most sensuous mouth. As she gazed at him, she found herself wondering what she would do if he tried to kiss her.

But he did not try to kiss her and nor did he touch her. In fact, though his expression was warm and friendly, he seemed deliberately to be keeping a distance between them.

Rachel tried to feel glad, but couldn't quite pull it off. Instead she found herself wondering about his outing last night—from which she'd heard him return just after two o'clock. Where had he and Kirsten gone? What had they got up to? And was he, she wondered, thinking about her now?

She found these questions troubling, though even more troubling was the fact that she was actually troubling to ask them.

Then Claudio suddenly stepped away. 'I think we should go and eat now. I don't know about you, but I'm famished,' he said.

It was only when at last they were outside in the street that Claudio took her arm and slid it through his. As Rachel tightened slightly, like a once-rejected lover, not knowing quite how to react to the sudden intimacy, he told her with a smile, 'Someone may be watching. So just grit your teeth and try to put on a good show again.'

Was that what *he* was doing, gritting his teeth? Rachel found herself wondering at frequent intervals throughout their lunch together as he flirted with her and encouraged her to tell him about her visit to the Uffizi. It was hard to tell. It all seemed to come so easily to him. He could switch on his seductive charms as if he were switching on a light. Even she at times was almost charmed into believing it was real.

But then again, when lunch was over and they went back to his studio for a coffee, his demeanour took on that friendly but distant feel again. Which is as it should be, Rachel told herself. Which is the way I want it, after all. Isn't that what I told him in the car last night?

Still, she knew that the promise she'd extracted from him last night was not what was causing this good behaviour on his part. No, he was behaving this way because he wanted to behave this way. Good, Rachel told herself. But it didn't actually feel good at all.

The only reason Rachel had gone back to his studio for a coffee was because everything was still shut for the afternoon siesta.

'You can waste half an hour or so at my place,' Claudio had suggested when she'd told him she wanted to do more sightseeing before catching the bus back to San Cappano.

He, for his part, was going to be busy.

'I've got a client coming at four-fifteen, then we've got to go out together,' he explained to her now as they sat at opposite ends of his huge desk drinking their espressos from tiny white cups. 'Otherwise I'd suggest we meet up somewhere later so that I could give you a lift back to San Cappano. The trouble is I'm afraid I don't know when I'll be free.'

'That's OK. I don't know how long I'll be either.'

Rachel shrugged, camouflaging the sudden awk- wardness she was feeling. She'd enjoyed their lunch, but since they'd come back to his studio she'd been suffering from the most ridiculous sense of anti- climax. It was this constant switching on and off be- tween intimacy and distance all the time. She just didn't know where she was any more, and she felt all bunched up inside with tension.

'I just want to look at the shops and maybe take in a church or two,' she elaborated. 'Then when I feel I've had enough I'll catch a bus back.'

She glanced at her watch. He'd said his ap- pointment was at four-fifteen and it was already after four o'clock now. She drained her coffee, put down her cup and stood up. 'I'd better go now before your client arrives.'

'I'll see you out.'

Claudio rose to his feet too, then led her across the studio and out to the lift. But, as the lift arrived and the lift doors opened, he did something that took Rachel totally by surprise.

Just as she was about to step inside, he reached out and caught hold of her and delivered the most delicious warm kiss on her lips.

'Have a nice afternoon,' he told her. 'I'll see you back at the villa tonight.'

And though it was totally ridiculous and utterly shameful Rachel felt her heart lift and the tension inside her vanish. That kiss hadn't been fake. It had definitely been real!

It was just after half-past six when Rachel got back to the villa and as she stepped into the hall the phone was ringing.

She paused for a moment, feeling an irrational plummeting inside her. I hope, she thought silently, it's not Kirsten or some other girlfriend. But as she picked up the receiver she was in for a shock.

'Darling, it's me. How are you getting on? I'm sorry I haven't managed to call you before.'

'Mother!' Rachel sank down on the chair by the telephone. I'm fine,' she began, 'but there's something I ought to tell you——' But before she could get any further her mother was cutting in.

'Look, I have to be brief, dear, so listen carefully to what I have to tell you.' Then she paused. 'Nothing's happened, has it? You did say you were all right?'

'Yes, I'm fine, Mother, but——'

'That's OK, then. Now listen very carefully, Rachel. I want you to do something very important for me. I want you to go to Dino's study and find a file that's in his desk there. It's a red file. It's in the top drawer. You can't mistake it. And then I want you to take it first thing tomorrow morning to the address I'm about to give you...'

She paused to snatch a breath. 'Do you have a paper and pencil handy?'

'Yes, I do.' There was a pad and pen on the phone table. Rachel pulled them towards her. 'But can I just explain——?'

'Later, darling. This is important.' Her mother proceeded to reel off a name and address. 'He's Dino's lawyer,' she explained, 'and he'll be expecting you. Now promise me you'll deliver the file first thing tomorrow?'

'I promise, Mother.'

'Good girl. You're an angel. Look after yourself, darling. I'll speak to you later.' And then she rang off.

Rachel sat for a moment, feeling a bit stunned, and stared at the name and address on the notepad. What was going on? What was her mother up to? And why was she being required to deliver a file to Dino's lawyer?

Still, there was really no point in wondering. She'd said she'd do it, so she'd better do it. And since she had the house to herself right now, perhaps she should go and dig out the file straight away. For she had a very strong feeling that this little task she'd been given was something that Claudio had better not know about.

She stuffed the name and address of the lawyer into her shoulder-bag then hurried upstairs to Dino's study.

Rachel had only ever set foot in Dino's study once before—when her mother had shown her round the villa on the day of her arrival. That seemed ages ago now, it struck her as she pushed the door open, even though in reality it had only been a couple of days ago. Who would believe so much could happen in such a short time?

Dino's desk was by the window. Rachel walked smartly over to it, but when she tried to pull open the top drawer she discovered it was locked. But the key was in the lock. With nervous fingers she turned it. All this secret agent stuff wasn't at all to her liking. She was just praying that the wretched file would be where her mother had said it was.

It was. With a sigh of relief she snatched it up. Mission accomplished, she thought to herself as she pushed the drawer shut and quickly turned the key. Now she would hide the file safely in her room till tomorrow.

But as she turned round to leave Rachel's stomach turned to lead. She froze to the spot, unable to move. For, standing in the doorway, watching her, was

Claudio, and the expression on his face was as cold as an Arctic winter.

He didn't move. He just fixed her with eyes like bayonets. Then he held out his hand and demanded, 'Now just give that file to me.'

CHAPTER FIVE

'I'll do nothing of the sort! This is none of your business!' Rachel hugged the red file protectively to her bosom. 'Now get out of the way and let me past!'

Claudio remained standing where he was.

'Give me the file, I said.' He eyed her threateningly from the doorway, his expression black, one hand still held out towards her. 'You either give it to me voluntarily or I shall take it,' he warned.

'By force, you mean?'

'I don't think much force would be required.' He smiled a dismissive smile as he looked her up and down. 'All the same, I would prefer it if you just handed it to me, now.'

'I've no intention of doing that.' Rachel hugged the file tighter, as though it were no less than the Crown Jewels she was protecting. 'This file is private. It's got nothing to do with you.' Her eyes flashed with fury. How dared he threaten her? He was nothing but an arrogant, odious bully!

But Claudio was about to cut the bullying short. Before she had time to dodge him, he had taken a step towards her and in one lightning movement had snatched the red file from her fingers.

'Thank you,' he said. 'So kind of you to co-operate.'

As Rachel stood there, fuming and silently debating whether she should try to snatch it back, he flicked it open and began studying its contents.

'These are all the legal papers connected with my sale of this house to Dino.' He flicked a curious, impatient glance at her. 'Would you mind telling me what you were planning to do with them?' he demanded.

Yes, she would mind. She would tell him absolutely nothing. Rachel glared back at him, her lips set in a tight, mute line.

But Claudio was capable of working things out for himself. 'My guess is that you were planning to take them to Dino's lawyer. He wasn't in on the deal, so he wouldn't have a copy.' He fixed her with a dark look. 'Am I right?'

Rachel still didn't answer, but her eyes betrayed her. Just for a moment they flickered revealingly as she stood there wondering why he had to be so damned clever. And Claudio, needless to say, picked up that tiny flicker.

He smiled a satisfied smile. 'So I'm right,' he concluded. 'No doubt they're hoping to track down some loophole in the agreement that will get old Uncle Dino off the hook. Well, they're wasting their time.' In a gesture of pure contempt, he tossed the red file on to the desk behind her. 'I come from a family of lawyers, remember? The agreements I draw up do not have loopholes.'

Then he narrowed his eyes at her and demanded, 'And on whose instructions were you planning to take the file to Dino's lawyer?'

Rachel ignored the question. She glared at him ferociously as she reached for the discarded file and snatched it up.

'I'd like to leave the room now,' she told him in a steely tone, for the way he was standing he was still blocking her exit. 'So perhaps you'd kindly get out of the way.'

'Once you've answered my question.'

Claudio didn't move a muscle. In fact, he seemed to position himself even more squarely in front of her, as solid and impassible as a piece of hewn rock.

'Who told you to take the file to Dino's lawyer?'

Rachel glared at him mutinously. You're so damned clever, she thought, why don't you work that one out for yourself as well?

But, even as she was thinking it, that was precisely what he did.

'It must have been either your mother or Dino. That's it. You received a letter or a phone call.' His eyes fixed her. 'So which of the two was it?' he wanted to know.

'I'm telling you nothing.' Rachel pinned her eyes on the doorway. 'And if you don't mind,' she repeated impatiently, 'I'd really like to leave.'

'My guess is it was a phone call.' Claudio smiled grimly down at her. 'That's what happened. You got a phone call when you got back, and, taking advantage of my absence, you sneaked off to get the file, intending to tell me nothing about it.

'That's very interesting.' His expression had grown harder. 'I'd really like to hear about this phone call.'

Then, to Rachel's astonishment, just as she was about to demand again that he move, he reached out and caught her firmly by the wrist, dragging her through the doorway and along the corridor.

'Let's go downstairs,' he ground out, 'and pour ourselves a drink, and you can tell me all about it.'

'There's nothing to tell!'

Still clutching the red file to her bosom, Rachel was glowering at Claudio from the depths of the green chintz armchair where he had dumped her just a couple of minutes ago. For he had half dragged her, half carried her downstairs to the sitting-room before depositing her unceremoniously amid the cushions with the growled warning, 'Don't even think of trying to run out on me until you've told me everything I want to know.'

Rachel smiled sourly to herself. She'd have a fat chance of escaping. Any attempt to do that would be a total waste of effort. All it would achieve would be to provide him with an excuse to bully her some more.

She rubbed her wrist, which was still smarting from the rough treatment it had received in the course of her ignominious descent down the stairs. 'Why are you so damned suspicious all the time?' she demanded. 'I'm not keeping anything from you!'

Claudio was standing by the drinks cabinet, pouring himself a whisky, but he paused now to cast her a disbelieving look. 'I can see this is going to take some time,' he observed disapprovingly. Then he indicated with a nod the array of bottles before him. 'Would you like a glass of something? It might help clarify your thoughts.'

'My thoughts don't need clarifying... but all the same I will have something.' If this was going to be a long session, a drink might be a useful anaesthetic. 'A vodka and tonic, if that's OK,' she elaborated.

'Ice and lemon?'

Rachel laughed. 'Ice and lemon? One minute you're dragging me about like a caveman and the next you're asking me if I want ice and lemon in my drink.' She threw him an amused look. 'You really are a one-off.'

'I'm glad you appreciate that fact.' Claudio proceeded to mix her drink, tossing in a couple of ice cubes and a slice of lemon before coming over to hand it to her. 'Since you didn't answer my question, I've assumed that meant yes.'

Rachel took the drink and watched him for a moment as he crossed to the sofa directly opposite her and sat down, stretching his long legs out in front of him. That remark about his being a one-off hadn't been intended as a compliment, but all the same as she found herself reflecting how true it was—he was utterly unique; she would never meet another Claudio—her feelings were a long way from being totally negative.

He drove her mad. There was no doubt about that. He was a bully and a womaniser. He had endless faults. And yet, for all that, there was something about him that made her feel more alive whenever she was around him than she had ever felt before in her entire life.

It was as though some spark in him set off some spark deep within her. Some spark she had never even known existed. *He's exciting*, she thought, wishing she hadn't thought it. *I never knew any man could be as exciting as this.*

She dropped her eyes and pretended to pour all her concentration into the simple act of laying the red file at her feet. Then she took a mouthful of her drink and spoke to herself sternly. She was an idiot to start thinking things like that.

'So. Let's get back to this phone call we were talking about . . .' Claudio's tone had resumed its earlier hard tone. 'Though perhaps, first, we should establish one essential detail—did they phone you or did you phone them?'

His tone of voice was the perfect antidote to her foolish feelings. Rachel snapped her gaze back up with a look of irritation. 'How could I phone them? I don't have their phone number, remember?'

'I remember that's what you told me. But who knows how true it is?'

Rachel sighed. 'It is true. Why won't you believe me?' Then she continued without bothering to wait for an answer, 'It was my mother who phoned me, just as you guessed it was. Just a short while ago. When I got in.'

'And how many phone calls have there been?'

'You mean from my mother?'

'From your mother or Dino.'

'None! That was the first one!'

'You're sure about that?'

'Of course I'm sure about it.' Rachel sighed with impatience. 'This is the first phone call I've had. There haven't been any others. And even this one only lasted a couple of minutes.'

Claudio took a mouthful of his whisky and surveyed her for a moment. 'OK,' he said at last. 'Tell me about it.'

'There's not much to tell. She just asked me to get the file and deliver it to Dino's solicitor first thing tomorrow morning.'

'OK. And what else was said?'

'Nothing.'

'Nothing?' One dark eyebrow lifted, clearly disbelieving. 'Surely you don't expect me to swallow that?' he said.

Rachel's fingers had tightened with irritation round her glass. Perhaps, she was thinking, he should have been a lawyer after all. He certainly had a lawyer's tenacity when it came to cross-examination! She sighed a deeply felt sigh. 'She asked me how I was.'

'And what did you reply?'

'I told her I was fine.'

'You told her you were fine? And then what else did you tell her?'

Rachel scowled at him. 'What do you mean?'

This time both eyebrows soared. 'Are you seriously trying to tell me that in the course of this conversation you failed to mention anything about us?'

Rachel flushed to her hair roots. He was right. It sounded incredible. 'I tried to,' she confessed, embarrassed, 'but she wouldn't give me a chance. Every time I tried to tell her she'd just interrupt me. She was in a hurry. She just wanted to tell me about the file and ring off.'

'This is quite extraordinary.' Claudio had leaned forward in his seat, every line of his body an accusation. 'To get your mother to listen, all you had to do was mention my name. Do you mean to say you didn't even do that?'

'No, I didn't.' She hadn't thought of that. 'I'm sorry,' she said.

'I thought you told me you were anxious to co-operate?' Claudio was watching her closely, his eyes flashing out his anger as he ground out the words. 'What the devil's going on here?' he demanded to know.

'Nothing's going on. I am anxious to co-operate. I want them to come back and for you to be gone as soon as possible.' Rachel scowled at him and demanded accusingly, 'Surely you don't actually think that I *enjoy* this stupid charade you're forcing on me?'

'Well, who knows? Maybe you are.' Claudio's tone was steely, in spite of a momentary lighter flicker at the back of his eyes. 'Here was the perfect opportunity to put an end to it and you're telling me that, just like that, you let it pass?'

'I tried.'

'I'll bet you did. Really hard, by the sound of things.' He narrowed his eyes. 'But surely you managed at least to get an address or a phone number out of your mother?'

Rachel shook her head glumly. 'No, I didn't,' she confessed.

'No?' This time Claudio sounded frankly astounded. He continued to fix her with dark eyes for a moment. Then he sat back in his seat. 'There's something going on here. You're lying. You're deliberately trying to protect your mother and Dino.'

Rachel felt something snap. She narrowed her eyes at him and sat forward in her seat with sudden belligerence. 'Well, maybe I am! Maybe that's precisely what I'm doing!' Suddenly, she'd had enough of being on the defensive. 'Good grief!' she exploded. 'I would say I deserve a medal for doing anything I could to protect them from a man like you!'

'They don't need you to protect them.'

'Maybe I think they do.'

'So you're admitting it, are you? There's something going on that you're not telling me about?'

'Maybe there is! Rachel sat up straighter to confront him. 'Maybe there's a hell of a lot going on that I'm not telling you about—nor have any intention of telling you about,' she added for good measure, 'no matter what bullying tactics you adopt!'

Claudio smiled. 'Brave words.' He drained his whisky glass. Then suddenly, abruptly, he rose to his feet, placing the empty glass with a sharp click on the low table beside him. 'Let's see how long it takes before you're forced to eat them.'

Rachel had shrunk back in her seat a little when he had stood up so unexpectedly. She'd half expected to be grabbed and the life shaken out of her, for there'd been a distinctly threatening glint in his eye.

But as he made no move to grab her, but instead stuffed his hands into his trouser pockets, almost as though he believed they might be safer there, and simply stood glowering blackly down at her, she felt brave enough to taunt him, 'You're not used to people standing up to you, are you? Everyone's scared of you. They just let you walk all over them. Well, you're in for a new experience, because I'm not the least bit scared of you, and I've had all the bullying from you I'm prepared to take.' She tilted her chin at him and shook back her bright red mane. 'So just lay off me and my mother and Dino!'

'I'll lay off you when I've finished with you, but I haven't finished with you yet.' The dark eyes flashed. He was as angry as she was. 'So if you want a fight, don't worry, you'll get one.'

Rachel didn't want a fight, but she forced herself to respond bravely, 'Good! I can't think of anyone I'd have more pleasure fighting!'

'Don't bank on that. On the pleasure bit, I mean.' Claudio smiled a dark, contemptuous smile down at her. 'When I fight, it's not for pleasure. When I fight, it's to win. That's where I get the pleasure. In winning.'

He started to turn away, then he paused and looked down at her. 'Talking about pleasure...' His tone was mocking. 'You and I are going to a party tonight. So be dressed up in your gladrags and ready to leave by ten o'clock.'

'A party? You're joking! How can we go to a party now?' Rachel laughed dismissively at the very idea. 'I couldn't possibly pretend to be madly in love with you tonight! Heaven knows, it's hard enough at the best of times, but tonight, I'm afraid, there's just no chance!'

'It is hard, I agree. But it's got to be done. Since you blew the perfect chance to get your mother and Dino back here, I'm afraid we'll just have to go ahead with our earlier strategy.'

He fixed her with a harsh look that brooked no argument. 'So be ready, if you don't mind, at ten o'clock precisely—and prepare yourself to put on the performance of your life.'

At ten o'clock precisely Rachel was dressed to kill in a pair of slinky red silk trousers and a skimpy red and black camisole top. Normally, she only ever wore the top beneath a voluminous silky overblouse, but what the hell? she'd thought. Tonight she'd pull out all the stops. For tonight she was really going to vamp it up, she'd decided. Tonight Claudio would have no sighing lovebird on his arm. Tonight what he'd have to contend with was a red-hot lover!

Only a fantasy one, of course, she smiled to her reflection as she slicked on just a little more red lipstick than usual and teased out her red curls into an exuberant halo. For she knew that was the only way she could pull it off tonight—by playing the whole thing over the top.

There was too much adrenalin shooting around in her system after that mean little set-to they'd had earlier on in the drawing-room for her to play the part of the meek, adoring girlfriend. If she couldn't sizzle with anger—which was really what she felt like doing—then she would simply have to sizzle with fake ardour instead!

Clearly, Claudio did not disapprove in the slightest of this development.

'Well,' he observed as she came sashaying through the sitting-room doorway, all bold, spiky edges, not looking at all as she normally did. 'It looks as though it's going to be an interesting evening.'

Rachel sensed it was too, and in a perverse way she was looking forward to it. She threw him a look of challenge, her eyes flinty, for she was still mad at him. 'You said you wanted the performance of a lifetime...' She swung her red shoulder-bag over her shoulder. 'OK,' she told him. 'Lead me to the party.'

The party was being held in a villa near Belvedere, and when Rachel and Claudio arrived it was already in full swing. Rachel looked around the room full of beautiful people, some standing in groups, laughing and chatting together, some dancing to the foot-tapping Latin American music that spilled out from the podium where the band was playing and on to the huge open terrace where even more guests were enjoying themselves. And she smiled, feeling a wonderful surge of energy.

This was precisely what she needed. A total lifting out of herself. To be in a place among people whose only aim for the evening was to have a totally uninhibited and thoroughly good time.

As Claudio led her into the throng, she gave a little shimmy and glanced at the dance-floor. 'Come on. Let's show them. Let's start dancing the night away.'

'I can see I'm going to have to keep a sharp eye on you tonight.' Claudio smiled at her, clearly intrigued by this new side he was seeing. 'But I'm afraid the dancing will have to wait for a bit.' As he spoke, he relieved a passing waiter of two tall flutes of champagne and handed one of them to Rachel. 'Before we start dancing, I think we ought to go and say hello to our hostess.'

'OK. Where is she? I want to congratulate her on all this.' Rachel cast an admiring glance round the fabulous room, all decked out with party decorations. She'd never seen anything quite like it in her life.

It was at that moment that a woman in a sparkly silver dress suddenly descended on them.

'Claudio, *tesoro*!' She kissed the air next to his cheeks. Then she turned to Rachel with an equally exuberant smile. 'Introduce me at once to this bird of paradise you've brought with you. My dear,' she told Rachel, 'you're the most gorgeous creature in this room.'

Rachel laughed as Claudio made the introductions, instantly liking the vivacious Anna, who, it turned out, was their hostess for the evening.

'It's a wonderful party,' Rachel told her. 'We've only just arrived and already I'm having a fabulous time.'

'That's what I like to hear.' Anna turned to Claudio and informed him, 'I like her. Not only is she stunning to look at, but I can see she's got a bit of spirit as well.'

She smiled at Rachel. 'That's the trouble with men. They're scared stiff of any woman with a bit of spirit. They're absolutely terrified they're going to be upstaged.'

Claudio laughed. 'Not Pippo, though. Surely he's an exception?'

'Of course!' Anna cast a quick glance round the noise-filled room till her eye fell on a man with a large bushy beard who was holding court to a group of delighted-looking guests. 'My beloved husband knows he's in no danger of being upstaged,' she laughed. 'And even if he was, he probably wouldn't notice.'

Then she continued, addressing the remark mainly to Rachel, 'Actually, young Claudio here's another rare exception.' She took his arm and squeezed it jokingly. 'That's why we get on so well together.' Then she pulled a face. 'His problem's a different one. His problem is——'

But she got no further, for at that point they were joined by another couple and the conversation swung off in a different direction. But Rachel was left feeling deeply curious. How had Anna been planning to finish that sentence?

They stood for a while and chatted with the others, but when the waiter came to offer them fresh flutes of champagne Claudio slipped an arm around Rachel's waist and told her, 'I think it's time we headed for that dance-floor. I can tell you're just itching to get out there.'

He was right. She was. As entertaining as the talk had been, Rachel was more in the mood for dancing than talking. Maybe dancing would help unleash all the tension inside her. For she was still keyed up and angry about the way he had treated her.

As he led her on to the dance-floor, she flicked Claudio a look of challenge. 'Now we'll see,' she told him, 'if you're any good as a dancer.'

Ten minutes later she was having to admit that he was. And what was more his style of dancing perfectly matched her own. It was quite disconcerting the way their bodies moved in perfect unison to the beat of the rumba the band was playing. Suddenly they were two people moving as one.

'You're not bad.' Rachel threw him a smouldering look of appreciation—strictly for the benefit of their audience! 'I mean not bad for a man with the soul of a bully.'

Claudio caught her and twirled her round as he answered, 'And you're not bad for an out-and-out liar.'

Rachel shot him a sharp look, disguised as flirtation. 'What was it Anna was about to say about you?' she demanded. 'She was about to tell us what she reckons to be your problem...'

Claudio's arm went round her waist as she executed another perfect twirl. 'I've no idea what she was about to say,' he purred back at her. 'However, I've no doubt it was something immensely flattering.'

'Hah!' Rachel scoffed, her fingers curling round his shoulder as, following his lead, she improvised a couple of deft steps across the floor. 'Well, you would think that, wouldn't you?' she told him crushingly. 'But, as it happens, I already know what your problem is.'

'Tell me. I'm curious.' He caught her and whirled her round.

'You're a pig and a rat.'

'And you, *cara mia*, are a total phoney.'

'There isn't an ounce of decency in you.'

They moved and wove to the music.

'And you wouldn't know what decency was if it jumped out and bit you.'

'Hah! Well, there's no danger of that happening with you around, is there?'

As they twirled and whirled around the dance-floor together not a soul could hear their *sotto voce* exchanges. Nor was anyone aware that every time Claudio spun Rachel towards him he tugged just a touch more sharply than was strictly necessary, just as every time she took hold of his hand she made a point of digging his flesh with her fingernails. There was a secret war going on out there on the dance-floor.

Yet neither of them, even for a second, missed a step or lost the rhythm. It was as though the beat and the music and the flying insults and their antagonism had all become one indissoluble part of the other.

And then suddenly the band broke into a tango.

Rachel smiled to herself as the lighter tempo of the rumba gave way to the more sensuous driven rhythms of the tango. This, she thought, is an even more suitable accompaniment, and she stamped her feet and flung back her head as she shot a dagger look across at Claudio.

'I hope someone of significance is watching this,' she snarled at him. 'I don't want to have to go through this charade again.'

And as they dipped and whirled and glided to the music Claudio was only too happy to keep up the barrage of abuse.

'You're not hoping it as much as I am,' he responded through his teeth. 'I don't think I could stand another evening in your company.'

It was more or less at that point that the two of them became aware that everyone else on the floor had stopped dancing. The crowd had fallen back and suddenly they'd become the focal point. Everyone was cheering them and clapping them as they continued their fierce tango.

Just for a moment Rachel was suddenly overtaken with nerves. Good grief, she thought, I'd no intention of becoming a floor show! But at the same time she felt a rush of heady excitement, and knew that she couldn't stop now, even if she'd wanted to. It was as though both she and Claudio had become lost in the rhythm, driven by the music, entangled in its spell.

And, though they continued to spit insults under their breath at one another, these too were now just another part of the excitement. The earlier underlying venom had gone.

'Pig!' Rachel shot at him as he caught her in a whirl.

'Cheat!'

'Womaniser!'

'Spoiled little brat!'

But as they caught each other's eye both of them were smiling. The combat between them had lost its

edge of anger and all at once had taken on an entirely
new complexion. They were still goading each other,
but not to battle. The air between them crackled and
sparkled with sex and humour. And Rachel suddenly
realised that she was laughing, her head thrown back
with sheer enjoyment. She had never felt so intensely
alive in her life.

And as they danced and danced and the music
throbbed and pounded Rachel felt quite tireless, as
though she could go on forever, as though her feet
and her spirit had suddenly sprouted wings.

Abruptly, the music ended and suddenly everyone
was clapping. 'Bravi!' 'Bravi!' 'Ancora!' they were
shouting. And as Rachel stood there, not knowing
quite how to respond, she was vaguely aware of
Claudio holding up his hands and laughingly remon-
strating. 'Later. Più avanti.' Then the music started
up again, this time in a gentle cha-cha, and the other
dancers were moving back on to the floor again.

Claudio took hold of Rachel's hand. 'We need a
drink after that.' And Rachel made no protest as he
led her off the dance-floor and through the crowd,
some of whom were still clapping and calling out,
'Bravi!' and patting them on the back as they passed.

He led her out on to the terrace, found two glasses
of champagne and told her, 'Let's go for a walk in
the garden. Unless you'd rather sit down for five
minutes?'

Rachel had no desire to sit down. Her heart was
still pumping furiously and she felt breathless and excited with energy to spare. 'No, I don't want to sit
down.' Though she wasn't at all sure what she did

want. But a walk in the garden seemed as good an idea as any.

There were lots of couples out on the terrace, either chatting or dancing. With Claudio in the lead, they made their way past them and down the stone steps that led to the garden.

'You're a star,' he told her, taking a mouthful from his glass and turning to smile at her as they headed along a gravel path. 'That was quite a performance back there.'

'The same goes for you. You're quite a star yourself.'

Rachel took a mouthful of champagne but did not look at him, for suddenly she was wondering if this walk was a good idea. All at once, she was acutely aware of his nearness and of the way he was holding her hand quite tightly, long, strong fingers laced with hers.

Not that it was an unpleasant awareness. If anything it was too pleasant. Just how pleasant it was was a little scary.

'Where did you learn to dance like that?'

'I took lessons,' she told him. 'I saw a film where everyone was dancing Latin American. I loved it and I thought it would be fun to learn.'

'With Mark?'

Rachel blinked at him. She almost said, with who? Then she bit her lip. 'No, not with Mark,' she answered. 'Mark isn't very keen on dancing. I went to lessons on my own.'

She stared down at the gravel a little confusedly for a moment. That mention of Mark had really thrown her. That part of her life suddenly seemed aeons away.

'Well, you learned well. You dance as though you were born to it.'

As he'd spoken, Claudio had slipped his arm round her waist and Rachel felt her heart give a helpless little flutter. 'Thank you,' she said, then, feeling suddenly dry-mouthed, she took a quick gulp of champagne.

She might have elaborated that she had never danced like that in her life before. It was all because of him and the way she'd found herself responding to him. Somehow he'd seemed to embody all the latent magic in the music. He and the music had made something in her soul come alive.

The strains of the cha-cha were drifting down to them from the house and Rachel could feel her heart beating in perfect tempo. 'We'll go back in a bit and dance some more,' Claudio was saying as they came, at the end of the path, to a sort of walled promontory with a spectacular view out over the countryside.

'That would be fun.'

Rachel leaned against the stone parapet and gazed down at the vista of hills and dark green cypresses. She wasn't really sure if she wanted to dance again. She felt oddly edgy. Even more keyed up than before. And it could never be as exciting again, she thought. To try to recapture that magic would just lead to an anticlimax. She sighed, trying to shake this strange edginess from her. It was the oddest sensation. She took another mouthful of her drink. Suddenly she just didn't know what to do with herself.

Then something caught her eye, distracting her for a moment.

She pointed. 'Look,' she said. 'What's that over there?'

Claudio was standing right behind her, his hand lightly on her waist. 'They're glow-worms,' he told her. '*Lucciole* in Italian. Haven't you ever seen them before?'

Rachel gazed at the tiny pulsating flecks of light, trying not to be conscious of the warmth of his hand. 'No,' she said, 'I don't think we have them in England. At least, if we have, I've never seen them. So I suppose we don't. I'd have seen them if we did.'

She was babbling and she couldn't help it. For it was quite impossible not to be conscious of the way he was touching her. Besides, making matters worse, he'd moved even closer. She could feel the hardness of his thigh brushing against hers, causing every single nerve-end in her entire body to start tingling.

And suddenly, to her astonishment and utter horror, she was filled with the desire to press herself against him. As he laid his glass on the parapet, she did the same with hers.

But she did not turn round. She did not dare to. Holding her breath, she kept her gaze fixed on the glow-worms that flashed and danced in the moonlight before them. 'What did you say they were called in Italian?' she asked him.

'*Lucciole*. Say it,' he bade her softly.

Rachel licked her dry lips. '*Lucciole*,' she repeated.

'Not bad.' Making Rachel shiver, he raised his hand slowly to curl beneath the hair around the back of her neck. And now there was an earthquake of sensations tearing through her, so intense, so violent she could hardly stand up straight.

She gasped for breath. 'I'm no good at languages,' she said tritely, wondering if she should throw herself Tosca-like from the rampart. It was the only way she could think of to escape. Though in truth she had not the remotest desire to escape.

'Nonsense,' he was saying. 'You just need more practice. Try saying it again. *Lucciole*,' he murmured.

Rachel could resist no longer. She turned to face him. '*Lucciol——*' she started to say, but she never finished the final syllable for, as she turned, he caught hold of her and with a sigh of impatience snatched her into his arms and kissed her.

CHAPTER SIX

WITH a little cry of surrender, Rachel fell into Claudio's arms.

I shouldn't really be doing this, she was thinking. But she could not stop herself and nor did she have any wish to. All she wanted was to abandon herself to his kisses, to sink into his arms, to feel their strength around her, to drink in the clean, masculine taste and scent of him.

And as his lips pressed against hers, firm and hungry, sending delicious tongues of red-hot flame shooting through her, she was aware that something quite extraordinary was happening. She had never felt anything even remotely like this before.

Her whole being, every inch of her from her scalp to her toes, was shimmering as though plugged into an electrical socket, and her heart was fluttering and dancing inside her as though she were caught on some magic rollercoaster. A sense of excitement so intense it left her breathless was charging through her like an unleashed whirlwind.

For there was something quite wonderful about the way he was kissing her. There was a heat and a hunger in the lips that devoured hers that made the tiny hairs on the back of her neck stand up. Yet at the same time that passion was tempered with gentleness, and somehow the combination was quite irresistible. The

urgency in him seemed to reach beyond the merely
sensual. It was as though he was reaching down into
the depths of her very soul.

Rachel found herself responding with joy and
longing, her hands sliding to his shoulders, pausing
to savour their muscular contours, before moving
round to caress the back of his neck softly. And her
lips quivered with delight as she traded kiss for hungry
kiss, shivering as her tongue collided with his, loving
the rough yet gentle scrape of his chin against her face.

Then he was cupping her breast through the thin
fabric of her camisole and a jolt went through her as
a fire leapt in her loins.

'*Lucciola mia bella*!'

He kissed the corners of her mouth, his hand gently
caressing her breast as he did so, grazing wickedly
against the hardening nipple.

Rachel moaned softly, feeling something jackknife
inside her. She sank against him, curling her fingers
in his hair, one hand moving down to press against
his chest, which felt as wonderfully hard as iron
against her spread palm.

And it was quite disgraceful, but as his fingers
moved up for a moment to caress the naked contours
of her shoulders and neck she was wishing that he
might slide away the strap of her camisole and let it
fall down loosely to expose her breast. She ached to
feel that hand possess her naked breast.

It was perhaps what he had intended to do, but to
her shameful dismay he did not. Instead he bent down
and kissed her shoulder, then paused to look into her
eyes for a moment.

'I think perhaps we ought to call a halt for now.' He smiled a regretful smile. 'After all, it's not exactly private here.' Then, softly and unhurriedly, he kissed her on the lips. 'Some things are better pursued in private.'

He pushed back her hair and looked deep into her eyes. 'I think we'd better go back to the party,' he told her. Then he took her hand and kissed her fingertips. 'Besides,' he reminded her, 'you promised me another dance, and if I'm not mistaken they're playing a fandango.'

Rachel raised her eyes from his and listened for a moment to the faint strains of music that drifted down from the house. It was funny, she thought, but she'd almost forgotten where she was. She'd felt locked in some private little dream world with Claudio. It was odd to remember that they were here at his friends' villa, set high up among the rolling hills of Tuscany— though, come to think of it, that was a pretty nice place to be, too!

She smiled back at him, suddenly feeling hugely happy with her lot. 'I don't know if I can do a fandango, but I'll try.'

Claudio laughed and hugged her, then kissed her hair. 'Anyone who can tango like you can certainly do a fandango. But if you can't, it'll be my pleasure to teach you.' He took her hand. 'Let's go and see.'

Something between them had altered. Rachel was vividly aware of it as they made their way back through the garden to rejoin the party. And it wasn't just that they'd stopped fighting, for somehow that was the least of it. Their relationship seemed to have shifted ground completely. It was as though each had taken a step towards the other, as though the barriers that had stood between them all at once had fallen.

Rachel felt suddenly moved to turn to him and tell him, 'You know, what I told you earlier was all absolutely true. About my mother, I mean. About the phone call. Nothing else was said. And I don't know where she and Dino are. I promise you. I hope you believe me?'

Claudio turned to glance at her as they reached the foot of the terrace steps. 'I thought you said you did know more?'

'I only said that because you made me angry, but I swear it wasn't true. Honestly,' she insisted. 'I've told you everything I know.'

'Are you absolutely sure?' He continued to hold her eyes. Then, unexpectedly, he smiled. 'Would I be wise to take your word?'

'You would be wise.' And suddenly Rachel could not resist it—that smile had sent something crashing inside her—she reached up very quickly and kissed him on the cheek. Then, blushing ever so slightly, she looked into his eyes. 'Please believe me. I promise you it is the truth.'

'OK, I believe you.' Claudio nodded and smiled and his fingers seemed to curl a little more tightly around hers. 'How could I not believe you on a magical night like this?'

Rachel was glowing inside as they climbed the stone steps. It really was true. All the barriers had fallen. All the anger and mistrust and antipathy had vanished. Suddenly there as a wonderful closeness between them.

And she wondered, as they crossed the crowded terrace hand in hand, if anyone was noticing the halo of happiness all around her. For she had never in all her life felt as stunningly happy as she was feeling at that moment.

They danced together until way after midnight. And though Rachel had been right when she had reflected earlier that it would be hard to recapture the same fierce excitement of before, the new intimate warmth and quite open sexual attraction that now simmered between them and poured unchecked from their eyes whenever they so much as glanced at one another was just as exciting and far more full of sensual promise.

Rachel found herself wondering with a squeeze of anticipation what was destined to happen when they got back home to the villa. And as her imagination took flight, her insides were tying themselves in knots.

Though I won't sleep with him, of course, she told herself firmly, a little shocked that the idea had even entered her head. To sleep with him tonight would be rushing things a bit.

Still, maybe it would just happen, she found herself reflecting as his lips grazed her hair, sending a rush of longing through her. Maybe, like a rollercoaster, there'd simply be no stopping it. Inflamed by fierce passion, perhaps they'd both be swept away.

At the thought she could feel her insides become all heavy. If that happens, it'll be pointless to try and resist. And why resist anyway? she asked herself dreamily. For Claudio, she knew, would be a wonderful lover. Surely the best possible lover for her very first time?

It was just after half-past midnight when he suggested, 'Shall we go?' His eyes seemed to search deep into hers for a moment. He squeezed her fingers softly and lifted them to his lips. 'I think I'd rather like to get back home—wouldn't you?'

Rachel nodded soundlessly, half afraid to look at him in case the longing in her heart might be revealed in her eyes. Suddenly the blood seemed to be rushing in her veins.

They said their farewells to Anna and Pippo and climbed without a word into the silver Maserati. And neither of them spoke much as they headed back to San Cappano. There just didn't seem to be any need for words.

Rachel was picturing in her mind how it was all going to happen.

He would lead her into the sitting-room, suggesting they have a drink. Then they'd sit together on the sofa and maybe chat for a few minutes—but then they'd look into one another's eyes and that would be the end of the chat. She shivered with excitement, imagining what would happen next.

A low moon was hanging above the red tiles of the villa as they drew up with a barely audible crunch of gravel. How beautiful, Rachel thought as she climbed out of the car.

'Look,' she said to Claudio. 'The moon's nearly full.'

He didn't answer. Perhaps he hadn't heard her, Rachel decided as she followed him up the steps to the front door. Perhaps he too was thinking about what was about to happen, for he had a vaguely distracted look.

She stepped into the hall behind him, expecting to be led to the sitting-room. But, to her surprise, in the hallway he turned to face her.

'I'm going straight to bed now. It's been a hard day,' he told her. His expression was distant and as cold as an ice-flow. 'So, if you don't mind, I'll wish you goodnight.'

Rachel was sure she'd gone quite pale and suddenly every inch of her felt frozen. She'd been expecting all sorts of things, but definitely not this.

Somehow, through stiff lips, she managed to say, 'Goodnight.'

Claudio started to turn away, heading towards the stairs. But then he paused to glance at her over his shoulder.

'I suppose we ought to have lunch again tomorrow. Just to make sure the message is getting through.' He sighed as though he found the entire business a nuisance. 'You'd better come to my studio around one o'clock.'

Then, suddenly a total stranger, he turned and hurried up the stairs.

Once in her room, Rachel closed the door behind her and remained standing for a long time, staring through the window, trying to figure out how she could have got things so wrong.

She'd misread all the signals. She'd fooled herself totally. Nothing had changed between them. It was all just like before. At the thought she felt sick and angry and ashamed.

Those kisses in the garden had meant nothing at all—and certainly not what she'd been foolish enough to think. And the new closeness between them had been nothing but a fantasy, a mere foolish invention of her overheated brain. He'd only kissed her, presumably, because he'd 'felt like it', just like last night after their dinner at the restaurant.

It was that tango that had done it. It had stirred him up a bit, just as, to be honest, it had stirred her up a bit, too. But that, very definitely, was where the comparison ended, for Rachel had been stirred because she'd been dancing with Claudio, whereas for him the identity of his partner had clearly been incidental. He would have reacted the same with any other girl.

That made her feel a little cheap and very angry with herself. She'd always known what he was like, that he enjoyed playing around with women, so how could she have dropped her guard so easily and behaved the way she had, with such total abandon? How could she have allowed herself to be so easily tricked?

With a scowl she crossed to the window and pulled the curtains to, shutting out the faintly mocking image of the moon. Well, one thing was for sure—it would never happen again.

*   *   *

If Rachel had had any reservations regarding her judgement of Claudio they would certainly have been laid to rest the following day.

After breakfast she took the same bus she'd caught yesterday into Florence. Claudio, to her relief, had already left when she'd got up. Then, after delivering the red file to Dino's solicitor—who was unable to provide any information as to Dino and her mother's whereabouts—she spent the rest of the morning sightseeing.

She visited the magnificent Duomo and the church of Santa Croce, stopping off at the famous leather factory there to buy some souvenirs and gifts to take home. And for a couple of hours she almost managed to forget Claudio as she lost herself amid the wonders of the city.

Almost, but not quite. For he had the disconcerting habit of springing into her mind when she least expected it. There she would be, gazing at some centuries-old statue, when suddenly she would realise her thoughts were miles away. She wasn't thinking of the statue—in fact, she wasn't really even looking at it. What she was doing was dreaming of Claudio and the way he had kissed her last night.

And it really was a disgrace to keep remembering his kisses, his kisses that she should never have allowed in the first place. Did she really want to be just another string on his bow, just another meaningless conquest for him to add to his list?

No, she did not, she told herself sternly as she finished her tour of the leather factory and stuffed her purchases into her bag. In fact, the very thought quite frankly appalled her. How could she ever have allowed herself to fall for such an odious man?

She glanced quickly at her watch and saw that it was just before one. It was time she started making her way to Via della Vigna Nuova. She mustn't forget their phoney lunch date!

Checking the route on her tourist map, she set off across the city, her steps decisive, her heart filled with resolution. Now that she'd got her head straight she'd have no trouble at all handling the situation with Claudio the way it needed to be handled. Last night was behind her and today's little pantomime—on her part as well as on his—would be one hundred per cent fake.

She reached the main door of the studio and was about to ring the brass bell when suddenly, as if by magic, it opened. A young man was stepping out, about to go off for lunch by the look of him. He must be one of Claudio's employees, Rachel decided, one of the admin people who worked on the floors below the studio.

She told him, as he hesitated about letting her enter, 'I've come to see Signor del'Angelo. He's expecting me.'

The young man smiled then. 'OK,' he told her, and stood aside to let her past. Then, just in case she didn't know, he added, indicating the lift, 'You'll find him on the top floor.'

Rachel stepped inside the lift and pressed the top button. She felt beautifully cool, calm and collected. Nothing Claudio could say or do could ruffle her today or cause her to act in any way unwisely. He wouldn't trick her again. She would play her part, but that was all. There'd be no more slip-ups. She was perfectly in control.

Besides, there couldn't possibly be any slip-ups, anyway—not now that she'd done such an excellent job of reminding herself just how much she disliked him.

Up on the top floor the lift glided to a stop and with a virtually soundless purr the lift doors opened. Rachel stepped out and crossed the short distance to the studio door, her knuckles raised, ready to deliver a sharp tap, when suddenly, almost like a replay of what had happened downstairs, as though of its own accord, the door swung open.

He hadn't been expecting her to be there and he didn't see her for a second. But Rachel, as she stood there frozen, could see him perfectly. And she could also see quite clearly the beautiful blonde at his side around whose waist his arm was wrapped as they laughed into each other's eyes.

As Rachel looked at them the floor beneath her feet fell away and the ceiling came crashing down on top of her head. All at once, she was incapable of moving a muscle.

Then Claudio spotted her.

'Ah, you've arrived,' he observed. His composure was perfect. He didn't miss a beat. With a smile he stood aside to let her pass into the studio—which she only just managed to do, on stiff, wooden legs. 'Just make yourself comfortable. I'll be with you in a moment.'

Then he stepped out to the lift, taking the beautiful blonde with him and discreetly half closing the studio door as he went.

And not for one moment, Rachel found herself observing sickly, had his arm left his smiling companion's waist.

Rachel was sitting out on the kitchen patio writing postcards. But though she'd been on the job for over an hour she was only halfway through her pile. She still hadn't fully recovered from lunchtime.

To her dismay, she'd found it very hard today to act the part of the loving girlfriend—she'd kept thinking of Claudio's arm wrapped round the blonde girl's waist—though, for once at least, Claudio had kept her agony short.

'If you don't mind, we'll just go and grab a pizza,' he'd told her, when at last he'd come back to join her in the studio. 'I'm a bit short of time. I have to see a client at two-thirty.'

'Why should I mind?' Rachel had tossed her response at him. The least time she spent with him the better, she'd thought. Especially right now. For she was absolutely fizzing.

Not that she had any reason to fizz. She kept trying to tell herself that. But it didn't help. She was fizzing all the same.

Claudio took her to a pizzeria down on the Lungarno—the street that ran along the side of the River Arno—though Rachel was rather disappointed that it didn't turn out to be the sort of quick takeaway place she'd been expecting. They sat at a bar table and shared a half-carafe of wine while the waiter took their order and cooked their pizzas on the spot.

'Are you sure you can spare the time?' Rachel asked him a trifle snippily. 'After all, I wouldn't want you to be late for your client.'

Who had the blonde been? she was wondering as she glared at him. And how many women, exactly, did he have? Her mother hadn't been joking when she'd talked about a legion!

Claudio was quite untroubled by her snippiness. 'Don't worry,' he assured her. 'I'll get back in plenty of time.' Taking a mouthful of wine, he glanced quickly round him. 'This place tends to get very busy at lunchtime. Someone's almost bound to see us.'

Quite illogically, Rachel felt insulted at that. He only ever took her places because of their charade. He only ever put his arm around her so that other people would notice. And the only occasions on which he kissed her were when he felt like amusing himself.

She was being totally irrational, but though she knew that it didn't help. And then, to her dismay, she heard herself saying, 'That girl back at the studio, was she a client?' And more shocking than the question was the tone in which she asked it. The words were touched not so much by irony as by poison.

Claudio swivelled round to meet her eyes and regarded her for a moment. 'A client?' he echoed. 'Why do you ask?'

Rachel glared down in wretched misery into her wine glass for a moment. She totally abhorred the way she was behaving, but somehow it was quite beyond her capabilities to stop herself from pouring out her poison. It was a bit like having a fishbone stuck in your throat. You couldn't relax until you'd coughed it up or it might end up choking you.

She tried to sound casual, but sorely doubted she was succeeding. 'I just wondered,' she said accusingly. 'After all, you didn't introduce me.'

Claudio smiled at the rebuke. 'No, I didn't. That was most remiss of me.' He drunk more wine. 'Her name's Lisa, since you're so interested.'

'I'm not "so interested",' Rachel scoffed. 'It just struck me as strange that you wouldn't introduce me to someone who was obviously such a close friend.'

'Was she obviously such a close friend?' Claudio shrugged and smiled, quite clearly enjoying himself immensely. 'I suppose you're right. But then,' he added with careless malice, 'most of my clients—at least, all the pretty ones—tend to be close friends.

'But don't worry,' he enjoined her as the waiter appeared with their bubbling pizzas. 'In future I'll be sure to remember my manners. I'll definitely make a point of introducing you next time.'

'Please don't give it another thought.' Rachel had seized her knife and fork and was setting about her pizza as though it were to blame for everything. Actually, she was simply grateful for the excuse to end the conversation. It had been getting a little out of hand and who knew where it might lead to? Especially with Claudio in the driver's seat.

And especially, she thought now, reflecting back on the incident, with herself for some reason so totally out of control. She'd been in danger of making an utter idiot of herself.

She took another postcard from her pile and stared at it for a moment. What on earth had got into her? She'd never behaved like that before. And where had all those fizzing emotions come from? The anger, the resentment, the sense of blind fury—and that feeling that knives were tearing at her insides?

It's just this whole situation, she told herself indignantly, starting to scribble a brief message on the back of the postcard. I hate being obliged to have anything to do with Claudio. I find everything about him absolutely odious. And, as if it isn't bad enough having to go through this charade with him, he starts flaunting his sexual conquests in my face. No wonder I got a bit upset!

But at least, compared to the previous day, their lunch had been brief.

'What are you planning to do now?' Claudio had asked her, pretending concern, as they'd left the pizzeria just after two-fifteen. 'Everything's still shut and nothing's going to open for an hour at least. If you like, you can come back and kill some time at the studio. I'm sure we can find an empty office where you can sit.'

'Thanks for the offer, but no, thanks,' Rachel had answered him. For she'd already decided what she was going to do, and it definitely didn't involve hanging around Claudio's studio. 'I'm going to take a walk up to San Miniato,' she'd told him. 'To see the church and admire the view.'

'It's a fair old walk, but it's worth it when you get there. OK,' Claudio had told her, 'enjoy your afternoon. I'll see you back at the villa this evening.'

He'd been right, it was indeed a fair old walk up to the magnificent eleventh-century church of San Miniato al Monte—reputed to have been Michelangelo's favourite church in Florence—and a large part of it was a pretty steep climb into the bargain. But he'd also been right that it was well worth the effort, Rachel had decided. No wonder it had been Michelangelo's favourite!

So Rachel had spent a thoroughly pleasant afternoon and had got back to the villa just after six o'clock. And now she was trying to get her pile of postcards written, though with her thoughts constantly straying in every direction she was making pathetically little progress.

Still, I am making *some* progress, she told herself, trying to be positive, as she stuck a stamp on the one she'd just written and added it to the somewhat meagre 'completed' pile. I'm getting there, slowly, she added, reaching for another one.

'So, you're out here, are you? I thought perhaps you hadn't got back yet.'

Rachel did not glance up, but her heart somersaulted inside her as Claudio spoke suddenly from the doorway behind her.

'I've been back for about an hour,' she said, bending in feigned concentration over her postcard.

'Writing to the folks back home, I see.' To Rachel's annoyance and dismay, instead of going back inside, he stepped out on to the patio and came to stand beside her at the table where she was sitting. 'Did you enjoy your trip to San Miniato?'

'It was lovely, thank you.' Rachel's tone was spiky. Why couldn't the wretched man just leave her in peace?

'I expect you went and had a coffee in the Piazzale Michelangelo afterwards?' As he spoke, he sat down on the spare chair opposite her. Simply to annoy her, Rachel felt positive.

'No, I didn't, as a matter of fact.'

She still did not look at him. The truth was, after she'd finished exploring the church, she'd done the natural thing and gone down to the piazzale, which was only a couple of steps away, intending to have coffee at one of the bars there. But suddenly she'd been assailed by the strangest sensations to find herself back in the very same spot where Claudio had brought her just two nights ago.

Her heart had started racing, she'd felt all dizzy and breathless, her feet suddenly heavy, as though dipped in wet cement. She'd taken one glance at the David, then had to snatch her gaze away. It was weird. She'd really felt most peculiar.

It must be the heat and the long climb, she'd tried to tell herself as she'd almost run to catch the bus that was about to leave the piazzale for the city. But she'd known that wasn't true. She'd long recovered from the climb. It was something else that had made her react in this strange way.

But as the bus had headed back down the winding *viale* to the Arno she'd preferred not to analyse too closely what it might be. Besides, as soon as the bus had started moving, she'd begun to feel a great deal better.

And now, keeping her head bent, she scribbled away at her postcard, fighting the memory of that moment in the piazzale.

'I'm busy,' she said, wishing Claudio would leave her. Couldn't he see she had no desire for either his company or his conversation? 'I'm trying to get through this pile of postcards.'

'So I see. Who are you writing to?'

Claudio was not discouraged in the slightest. He was impervious even to hints as broad as a barn door.

'To my sisters, to my friends, to people at work.' Rachel rattled off the list with unconcealed irritation.

'And who is that one to—the one you're writing now? You seem to have quite a lot to say in that one.'

Rachel paused for a moment and stared at what she'd been writing. This postcard was for her friend Abigail—though she hadn't addressed it yet—and, as always, for Abigail liked newsy postcards, she'd packed in twice as much as on any of the others.

But on an impulse she glanced up and told him in a tight tone, fighting the thrust to her heart as she looked into his eyes, 'Since you're so curious, this one happens to be to Mark.'

'Mark? Your boyfriend?' He smiled as he said it. 'So what have you been writing to Mark?'

'This and that. The usual sort of stuff.'

Rachel swallowed. Her mouth felt suddenly quite dry and her heart seemed to have lodged in her throat and stopped beating. It had all happened the very instant she had looked into Claudio's eyes and it was a feeling not unlike the one that had afflicted her in the piazzale. All at once, she felt quite breathless and most peculiar.

Quickly, oddly panic-stricken, she detached her eyes from Claudio's, trying to suppress these overpowering feelings. And trying, too, to ignore his suddenly amused expression that, on top of everything else, she found quite distressing. She'd only said the postcard was for Mark in order to put him in his place, to underline the fact that he meant nothing to her. But he didn't look put in his place. It was clear he couldn't care less.

'This and that?' In a mocking tone, he repeated what she'd just said. A short pause, then he asked, 'Have you told him about us?'

'Us?' She glanced up at him again, her expression carefully composed. 'What is there to tell about us?'

'Our arrangement. Surely you've told him about that?'

'I don't think that's necessary. I'll tell him when I see him. There's no point in going into all the boring details now.'

'He'll find them boring, will he?'

'I shouldn't think they'll be of much interest.' Rachel was wishing he would end this interrogation. 'After all, it's nothing but a stupid charade.'

'Maybe. But if I were in his shoes I'd definitely want to be informed. In fact, I'd be as mad as hell if I wasn't.'

As he spoke, he reached out idly for her pocket address book that lay on the table near where he was sitting and riffled the pages as one would riffle a pack of playing cards. Not for one instant did his eyes leave her face.

Then suddenly he smiled, a look of knowing challenge in his eyes. 'But I know why you haven't told him,' he announced. 'You haven't told him because he isn't really important. He's just a casual boyfriend. Go on, admit it. I know I'm right. You're not seriously involved.'

So that was what he thought? Rachel blinked back at him for a moment. Well, it explained why any mention of Mark never seemed to bother him. Though that was a laugh. Why would it bother him? He didn't care for her, after all. All he enjoyed was fooling around with her.

Rachel felt a clench inside her. There must be no more fooling around, and maybe if she'd been a bit more convincing about Mark from the beginning, maybe if she'd behaved as though she really did have a boyfriend back home, there might not have been any fooling around in the first place. She straightened her spine. It was time she got her act together.

'You're totally wrong, you know. Mark is anything but a casual boyfriend.' She was rather pleased at the note of calm authority in her voice. 'Mark and I,' she added, 'have known each other for years.'

'Years?'

'Yes, years.'

'That's very interesting.' There was a pause as again
he riffled the pages of the address book. 'And I'm
wrong, you say? It's not just a casual affair?'

'Yes, you're totally wrong.' Rachel regarded him
steadily. Not a flicker betrayed this fabrication she
was feeding him. Self-preservation had taken over. She
had to do it. 'As a matter of fact,' she said, 'I'm
planning to marry him.'

'Marry him, indeed? Well, that's a turn up, if you
like.'

Just for a fleeting second, a shadow seemed to cross
his eyes. Something seemed to darken way back in
their depths. But a split-second later Rachel knew she
had imagined it as he smiled and tossed the address
book over towards her.

'In that case, I hope you'll both be very happy.'
Then, surprising her, he stood up and completely
changed the subject. 'So tell me, what are the plans
for tonight?'

Rachel gave an impatient snort as she turned her
attention back to her postcard, trying to control the
way her heart was rushing inside her. Never in her life
before had she told such a monstrous lie. 'I've no
doubt,' she said calmly, 'you have some little torture
planned. I suppose you're expecting us to continue
with our charade?'

That was something that, fatalistically, she'd taken
for granted.

But Claudio surprised her again.

'No, I'm not, as a matter of fact.'

'Really? That's good news.' Rachel glanced up at him.

He smiled in response. 'I thought you'd be pleased.' Then, watching her, he added, 'Here's some even better news. I won't even be around to get in your hair. You'll have the villa all to yourself tonight. You see, I have a dinner engagement elsewhere.'

With that, he glanced at his watch, then headed for the door. 'I'll go and get ready now and leave you to your postcards.'

Rachel couldn't have been more happy with this arrangement. At least, that was what she told herself as she struggled through her postcards. For her mind just wasn't on what she was doing. Who was he going out to dinner with? she was wondering.

Someone pretty special, she found herself concluding when, just over half an hour later, he walked into the kitchen where she was searching in the freezer for a TV dinner.

He was wearing a mid-blue suit, beautifully cut, with a perfect white shirt and a red tie at his throat. And there was only one way to describe him. He looked utterly stunning. He seemed to illuminate the very air around him.

Similarly, there was only one way to describe Rachel's feelings as she stood there by the open freezer and looked into his face. She felt totally demoralised and sick to her soul.

'I just came to say I'm off.' He smiled. 'Don't wait up for me. I don't expect to be back until rather late.' Then he turned on his heel and started to leave.

Perhaps it was that taunting 'Don't wait up' that caused Rachel's reaction. Or perhaps it was just the too pleased smile on his face. But, just as he was about to disappear, she found herself calling after him accusingly, 'You're having dinner with that blonde girl— the one who was at your studio. Aren't you?'

Claudio paused and turned to look at her. 'No, as a matter of fact, I'm not.' He looked a little surprised by her outburst.

Rachel was surprised too. She was also horrified and shocked. But, in spite of all that, she didn't stop.

'It's some woman, though, isn't it? You're having dinner with some woman. Who is it?' she demanded. 'Is it Kirsten?'

'No, it's not Kirsten either. But you could be right about it being a woman. After all, as you know, I enjoy the company of women.' Then he looked into her face and demanded with raised eyebrows, 'So what's the matter? You appear to have some objection.'

Rachel was overwhelmed by shame at what she was doing. As she looked back at him, she could see the amusement in his eyes and knew that he had every right in the world to look amused.

She tried to salvage the situation. 'I have no objection. It's just that I feel it's probably not a good idea for you to appear in public with another woman when you're supposed to be pretending to be having an affair with me.'

As an argument, it almost sounded half reasonable, but her tone was so brittle she could scarcely get the words out.

'So that's what's worrying you?' As his smile grew broader, Rachel sensed that he knew very well that that was not what was worrying her at all. 'Don't think twice about that,' he assured her. 'This won't harm our little charade. Everyone knows what I'm like—that I never have just one woman at a time. All this will do is add a bit of spice.'

Then he glanced at his watch. 'I'd better not be late.' A moment later he had disappeared out into the hall.

Rachel stood there for a moment, utterly appalled at herself. Why had she done that? What had got into her? How could she have demeaned herself by questioning him that way?

She didn't care whom he was having dinner with. It didn't matter a damn to her. He could have dinner with every girl in Tuscany for all she cared!

She slammed the freezer door shut.

'I hate him!' she seethed.

Then she covered her face with her hands and burst into tears.

CHAPTER SEVEN

It was a good ten minutes before Rachel stopped sobbing. She just stood there, her heart aching, her hands covering her face, and wept with huge sobs, the tears rolling down her cheeks. Then she stumbled upstairs, collapsed on to her bed and sat staring unseeingly at the plain white wall. Never in her life before had she felt so totally wretched.

And there was no point in denying it any longer. These symptoms she was suffering could add up to only one thing.

The rush of fierce emotion each time she looked into his face. The way she responded to his kisses. These feelings that had overcome her this afternoon in the piazzale. Her disappointment last night when nothing had happened after the party. And now this overwhelming jealousy. Unbearable, uncontrollable. Like knives slashing inside her.

She'd tried to deny it, but she could deny it no longer. Somehow, disastrously, she'd fallen in love with Claudio.

Rachel sighed and fell back against the embroidered cotton coverlet. How could it have happened? She must be crazy. Falling in love with a man like Claudio was a one-way ticket to misery.

She covered her face in despair. She should have seen it coming. She should have done something to stop it before it got this far. For it was too late now. This wasn't love in the early stages. This was fierce and overwhelming. This was the real thing. Like being eaten up by fire and then reborn all over again. After this, she could never be quite the same again.

Rachel closed her eyes and let her misery wash over her. Wasn't love supposed to be joyful? Uplifting? Happy? Wasn't it supposed to make your heart soar and your spirits sing?

Yes, she thought, if you fall in love with the right man. But trust me to fall in love with the wrong one. Trust me to condemn myself to a future without hope.

A tear slid down her cheek and melted into the bedspread. It was ironical in a way. All these things she felt for Claudio were the very things that had been missing in her relationship with Mark. That special spark. That touch of magic. That indefinable something that made the blood quicken in your veins.

She sighed a bitter sigh. Well, she'd found all these things now. And what good were they doing her? None, she thought miserably. All they were doing was tearing her heart to pieces.

With a sob she rolled over and buried her face in her arms. How could you? she berated herself. How could you do it? How could you be so mad as to fall in love with a man who you know is incapable of loving you in return?

Why, he'd admitted it himself—that he was a philanderer and a womaniser. And she shivered as she remembered, word for word, what he'd said tonight. 'Everyone knows what I'm like—that I never have just

one woman at a time.' And this was the man she'd
lost her heart to.

And now? she wondered. What was happening now
on his dinner date? She closed her eyes tightly. She
dared not think of it. To think of it was to feel as
though she was dying.

With a helpless cry she pounded the bedspread,
wishing with all her heart that it were Claudio beneath her fists.

About an hour later Rachel pulled herself together.

He wasn't worth it, she told herself. And she didn't
deserve all this agony. She would take a shower, then
go downstairs and have something to eat.

Dressed in her blue-flowered robe, she went down
to the kitchen and poked around in the fridge for inspiration. And though she wasn't really hungry—her
appetite had evaporated—she piled some cheese and
tomato salad on to a plate and went out on to the
front veranda to eat it.

The moon was full, shining down its silvery beams
on to the cypress-green hills and olive groves beyond
the garden. Rachel chewed on a tasteless mouthful
and stared at the landscape. It seemed particularly
miserable to be miserable in such a place. It was a
place made for happiness and joy and peace of mind,
not for the wretchedness she was feeling. But how
could she not be wretched, knowing what Claudio was
up to? She felt the tears well up again, but forced
them back. She refused to cry another single tear
for him.

And it was at that moment that the phone inside the house began to ring.

Rachel laid down her fork and got to her feet, then made her way unhurriedly through to the sitting-room. If it was one of Claudio's girlfriends, she'd get very short shrift.

She picked up the phone. 'Hello?' she said. And then she very nearly dropped the receiver.

'Rachel! What have I been hearing about you and Claudio?' It was her mother and she sounded close to apopleptic. 'Tell me it's not true! My God, I can't believe it! My own daughter! Rachel! What's been going on?'

Rachel tried to remain calm, but her heart was suddenly racing. The minute her mother had said his name she'd felt a jolt of love and pain.

'What are you talking about?' she answered, feeling anxious and confused.

'What am I talking about? I'm talking about all these stories I've been hearing. About you and that reprobate nephew of Dino's.' Poor Emily could hardly speak for emotion. 'I've been told you were seen at a party together behaving in a most undignified manner. You've been seen having dinner. I'm told you've even visited his studio.' She sounded in despair. 'Rachel, what's going on?'

'Nothing's going on.' But there was a crack in Rachel's voice. A crack of regret and pain and disappointment. It was a most unconvincing-sounding denial.

'There *is* something going on!' Her mother had picked up that waver. 'Oh, Rachel, what's he been doing to you? Oh, my God, this is terrible. It's even worse than I suspected!' Before Rachel could say a word, she hurried on and told her, 'Look, we're coming back at once. Don't do anything until we get there. We should be back tomorrow afternoon at the latest.'

'There's no need for you to rush back.' Rachel sensed she shouldn't be saying this. The plan, after all, had been to lure her mother and Dino back. But she wasn't thinking very clearly. 'No need at all,' she insisted.

Her mother was paying her no heed anyway.

'No need?' she echoed in horror. 'There's every need! You appear to have taken leave of your senses! So just stay put and we'll see you tomorrow. And in the meantime please try to stay out of that man's clutches.'

Well, there's no problem there, Rachel reflected a little bitterly as she laid down the phone and stared at it for a moment. Then she sighed. It would appear that Claudio's little trick had worked—in spite of her own rather dubious performance on the phone right now. Good, she told herself. That would be the end of her ordeal. Now she could just concentrate on getting him out of her mind—a task she could never have accomplished if he'd continued to hang around. Though she suspected that, even once he'd gone, it wasn't going to be easy.

She went back outside and picked at her salad, then sat staring at the moon as she poured herself some wine. She would wait up for him, she decided, and give him the good news. No doubt he would be even more delighted than she was.

Midnight came and went and there was still no sign of him. Rachel poured herself more wine. Well, she hadn't expected him to be early. She stared at the moon, which had gone a little blurry, and tried very hard not to imagine what he might be up to.

I don't care anyway, she told herself. He can do as he pleases. When it comes down to it, nothing could matter to me less.

And it was at that moment that she heard a low, familiar growl as the silver Maserati came crunching down the driveway. Quite unconsciously, Rachel found herself squaring her shoulders and taking another quick mouthful from her glass. Suddenly her heart was beating very fast.

Claudio climbed out of the car and started to come towards the house, carrying his blue suit jacket over his arm. And Rachel watched him, knowing he couldn't see her, for she hadn't switched on the veranda light and was sitting in almost total darkness. And it was utterly foolish how fiercely her heart was knocking against her ribs.

Just the way he walked—that easy upright carriage, the forceful silhouette, those broad shoulders, the long legs... She felt something trip inside her, a huge rush of emotion. It was only a few hours since last she'd seen him, but still it was wonderful to see him again.

And then suddenly he spotted her, just as he was about to head for the front door. He turned and climbed the steps to the veranda instead.

'Why are you sitting in the dark?'

'I didn't bother to put the light on.'

'Yes, I can see that.' He stepped past her quickly and flicked the switch just inside the veranda door. 'There, that's better. Now we can each see who we're speaking to.'

Rachel wasn't sure she wanted to see him that clearly. She blinked at the sudden light, took a mouthful of her wine and carefully kept her eyes averted.

'Did you have a nice evening?' she asked him.

'Very nice indeed, thanks.' Claudio proceeded to seat himself in one of the chairs that were arranged round the little table where Rachel was sitting, tossing his jacket over the back of another one. Then he sat back and looked at her. 'And you?' he asked her. 'Did you have a pleasant evening as well?'

'I had a terrific evening.' Rachel tilted her head and smiled at him and she was rather pleased at the light tone of voice she had achieved. It was all the wine she'd drunk. It made her feel less vulnerable. In celebration, she took another mouthful.

'I'm glad to hear it.' Claudio was slipping off his tie and tossing it over the back of the chair beside his jacket. 'I was a little worried you might be bored on your own.'

Yes, I'll bet you were! Worried silly! Rachel thought it but did not say it. There was no need to say it. They both knew it was a shameless fiction. Instead she informed him, 'Why would I be bored? Only people with very poor inner resources get bored when they spend time on their own.'

Claudio smiled at that. 'I see,' he responded. 'So poor inner resources are not an affliction you suffer from?'

'Far from it. On the contrary, I rather enjoy my own company, I have an extremely rich and fertile inner life.'

Rachel smiled to herself, feeling really rather impressed at the way she was getting her tongue round all these polysyllabic things she was saying. For she had realised as soon as she'd started speaking that the bottle of wine she'd consumed over the course of the evening had very definitely had an effect. It seemed to have twisted up her vocal cords just a little. She had to concentrate very hard every time she spoke.

She was concentrating very hard now as she told him, 'Not all of us have to go out partying all the time, indulging in meaningless social contacts in order to give our lives spurious meaning.'

'Is that a fact?' Claudio was still smiling—though whether he was laughing at her or with her Rachel wasn't quite sure. She didn't care anyway. She just smiled back at him as he added, 'I hadn't realised you were such a philosopher.'

'No, I expect you hadn't.' Rachel flicked him a cool look—well, as cool a look as she could manage in her inebriated state. 'I expect you also don't know why I went to the trouble of waiting up for you?'

Claudio raised one amused eyebrow. 'You mean it wasn't just to welcome me home?' He feigned a look of disappointment. 'Well, now, that's a bit of a blow.'

Sarcastic pig! But Rachel let his sarcasm wash over her. She was too busy thinking something else. For it had suddenly struck her that she hadn't quite been honest with herself when she'd decided to stay up and wait for him to come back. She'd told herself it was just to pass on the news about her mother's phone call, but that hadn't really been the reason at all.

The real reason, she realised, had been so that she could check up on him. She'd wanted to see how he looked after his night out. Would his hair be dishevelled? Would his clothes be crushed and wrinkled? Might there even be some tell-tale mark of passion on his person—like the scratch of a long fingernail or a smear of lipstick on his face? She had known she wouldn't sleep until she had seen him.

Only now she wasn't sure how to interpret what evidence there was—the shed jacket, the loosened tie, the undone buttons of his shirt. After all, it was a warm night. There could be an innocent explanation.

There could also, of course, be a far less innocent one. And it was this latter possibility that had instantly sprung to her mind as she had watched him climb the steps to the veranda—though these suspicions had proved not nearly as wounding as she'd expected.

The reason for that, she knew, was the quantity of wine she'd imbibed. It had had a wonderfully soothing, anaesthetising effect.

She looked at him now, rather enjoying her state of untouchableness, though rather wishing that his features wouldn't keep drifting out of focus.

'You flatter yourself,' she said with a nice edge of amused contempt. 'The only reason I stayed up was because I have something to tell you.'

'Oh?' As he smiled at her, he undid another shirt button. 'In that case, hadn't you better tell me what it is?'

Quite involuntarily, Rachel's eyes had drifted to his shirt-front and to the row of undone buttons that revealed a generous portion of his chest. She had seen it all before, of course, but it drew her just the same. It was so smooth and dark and she longed to lay her hand against it.

She snatched her eyes away. 'My mother phoned,' she said.

Ah. Now he was interested. One curved black eyebrow lifted. He moved ever so slightly forward in his seat.

'And what did your mother have to say?' he enquired.

'She's heard all about us. It's got back to them, it seems.' Rachel omitted the details of her mother's outrage. She suspected he would only find such details flattering. 'They're coming back at once. They'll be here tomorrow afternoon.'

'So it worked.' Claudio smiled—though just for a moment Rachel thought she saw the strangest look cross his face, almost as though he had some secret reservation. I must have imagined it, she decided. After all, my vision's a little unsteady. And that seemed to be borne out as he assured her, 'Well, that's good news.'

'Yes, I thought you'd be pleased.'

'It's the best news I could have hoped for. The perfect end to a perfect evening.' He glanced at his watch. 'And now I think it's time for bed. Tomorrow, I suspect, is going to be a busy day.'

He began to rise to his feet. 'Are you going to turn in too?' He cast a glance at the empty bottle on the table. 'You may as well. After all, you've drunk all the wine.'

Rachel was thinking the same thing—that it was time she turned in. All at once she felt so sleepy, it was hard to keep her eyes open and she was certainly quite beyond continuing their conversation. She wasn't even very sure what he was saying any more.

She nodded. 'I think I will.' And she began to rise to her feet. And that was when she very nearly toppled over.

But in the very same instant that she seemed about to crash to the floor, taking the table and its contents with her, Claudio caught hold of her and drew her upright.

'You appear to be a bit the worse for wear,' he told her, slipping his arm around her waist. 'Come on. I think you'd better let me help you.'

Rachel did not argue. She sank gratefully against him as he began to lead her through the veranda doors. But even with his help she was having difficulty making her legs move. Her feet seemed to be scuffing at random across the floor.

She giggled. 'I'm sorry. I don't seem to be able to walk.'

'No, you don't.' Halfway across the sitting-room, Claudio paused for a second. Then, before Rachel knew what was happening, he had swept her up into his arms. 'Lean against my shoulder,' he instructed her. 'Put your arms around my neck.'

Rachel did as she was told and sighed with pleasure as he began to carry her effortlessly across the room. She allowed her head to sink against his shoulder and the blood was suddenly rushing with warm excitement in her veins as she drank in the medley of cool, erotic scents that was suddenly pouring into her nostrils.

They were the scents of him, of his skin and his aftershave, and they were all so deliciously familiar and soothing. And so intoxicating that suddenly she could not resist it. With a little sigh, she reached out and kissed him on the cheek.

They were out in the hall now and approaching the staircase, though Rachel was not paying the slightest attention to their progress. Instead, as she continued to caress his cheek with her own, one hand slipped down to the open front of his shirt and, entirely of its own accord, slipped inside. Her palm pressed against the warm flesh, wondering at its strength and its hardness, her fingers trickling through the sprinkling of silky dark hairs.

'Mmm!' she murmured with a little giggle against his cheek.

They had reached the top of the stairs and were heading along the corridor, just as Rachel was starting to undo the rest of his shirt buttons. And suddenly her breathing was sharp and erratic as she nuzzled her lips against his neck.

'You taste delicious,' she told him, taking a little nibble. And he did. He tasted like nectar on her tongue.

Rachel was still partaking of this delight when he pushed open her bedroom door, switched on the light and headed towards the bed. 'Here we are,' he told her, laying her on it. 'Now I suggest you get some sleep.'

'Not yet.' Rachel's arms were still wound round his neck. She kissed his chin as she dangled there and giggled again. 'I don't want to sleep. I'm not sleepy in the least.'

'I think you'll find you are if you just close your eyes.' Claudio was smiling as he reached up to disentangle her arms. 'Now be a good girl and just go to sleep.'

'I don't want to be a good girl.' As he continued to bend over her, with a wicked little smile Rachel reached up and kissed his naked chest. Hazily, she looked into his eyes. 'Mmm. That was nice.'

'I'm sure it was.' He was still smiling down at her as he lifted her up for a moment to pull back the coverlet. Then, laying her down again, he invited, 'Now just get under there and go to sleep.'

'Only if you come under too.' Rachel giggled again. She was no longer sure what exactly was going on—her own voice and his seemed to come from far away. But, whatever was going on, she was thoroughly enjoying it. And there was one thing she was quite sure of. She didn't want him to leave.

But he was shaking his head and starting to straighten away from her.

'No!' Rachel protested. Then she glanced down at her robe. 'I can't sleep in this!' She pulled at the front with fumbling fingers. 'This is a robe. This isn't for sleeping in!'

'Then take it off, if you like.'

'I can't. You take it off for me.' She sank back on the pillows, inviting him to disrobe her. 'Go on,' she insisted. 'I can't sleep in this!'

Claudio sighed, then shook his head. 'OK, if you insist.' He reached down to undo the belt at her waist, then made her sit up so that he could slip the robe from her shoulders. A moment later, it slid away to reveal her naked breasts, firm and full and aching for his caress. Then the entire front of the blue-flowered robe fell open and he found himself looking down at her creamy-skinned thighs, the soft, womanly curves of her waist and stomach and the neat little triangle of silky red hair.

Rachel laughed. 'You didn't know I had nothing on underneath!' She reached up once again to slide her arms round his neck, longing to draw him down beside her. 'Let me undress you now,' she mumbled, fumbling with his shirt. Every inch of her was aching to feel his naked flesh against hers.

But Claudio was shaking his head, a little more firmly this time, and though the smile had gone the look in his eyes was kind.

'No,' he was saying. 'Some other time perhaps.'

Then carefully, almost lovingly, he pulled the coverlet over her, pushed back her hair and bent to kiss her cheek.

'Goodnight, *amore bello*. Sleep well,' he said.

There was something so soothing about those musical tones that Rachel smiled and closed her eyes.

And, before she could open them again, she was sound asleep.

Rachel awoke next morning with only a vague recollection of what had happened.

She lay for a while and stared at the ceiling. Claudio had carried her upstairs. She remembered that much. And somehow—though this bit was vague—she had got into bed. She had also undressed. That was clear, since she was naked. But whether she had undressed herself or Claudio had undressed her she really hadn't the vaguest recollection. And had anything else happened that she didn't remember? she wondered.

She pushed these thoughts away, unable to deal with them for the moment. For she had a much more pressing concern—her poor aching head.

'I have to get some Alka Seltzer.' She sat up and reached for her robe, feeling the whole room lurch sideways at the sudden movement. Someone with a pickaxe seemed to be chipping at the inside of her skull.

Oh, lord, she thought, how could I have done it? How could I have sat there and drunk a whole bottle of wine?

She didn't dare glance at her reflection in the dressing-table mirror as she crossed the room and headed downstairs. No point in giving herself a fright, she decided, and besides, she was in a hurry to get to the kitchen. She had a feeling she'd seen some Alka Seltzer down there.

But that wasn't all she found. To Rachel's dismay, Claudio was sitting at the breakfast-table.

He was fully dressed, wearing a white shirt and light trousers, and he glanced up from his brioche and cup of frothy *caffelatte* as she stopped dead in the doorway at the sight of him.

'I didn't expect you down so soon.' He tossed a smile at her. Then, seeing the grey look on her face, he nodded towards the cupboard in the corner. 'You'll find the Alka Seltzer in there,' he told her.

Rachel headed blindly for the cupboard, though suddenly she'd forgotten her headache. Instead she was remembering why she'd drunk that bottle of wine. It was because of him. Because of what he did to her. It was because of these feelings she couldn't control.

And now, just one look into his handsome, dark-eyed face and her heart had started dancing a tango in her chest. Feeling weak with misery, she pulled open the cupboard door. That's why I drank a whole bottle of wine, she told herself. Because I love him, and because he doesn't love me.

Keeping her back to him, she crossed to the sink and poured herself a glass of water, then dropped in a couple of tablets and watched them fizz.

'Surely it's not like you to have breakfast here,' she commented, her tone accusing, almost resentful, as though she might persuade him just to get up immediately and leave. 'I thought you always had breakfast in some bar near your studio?' That was what he'd told her once.

'Normally, I do, but I'm not going into the studio today. In view of what's about to unfold this afternoon, I thought I'd better be ready and waiting. Besides,' he added, smiling, 'it's a little late to go into work.'

Rachel hadn't even bothered to look at the time, but she turned now and glanced at the clock on the wall.

'Good heavens!' she exclaimed. 'I had no idea it was so late.' For, to her astonishment, it was almost a quarter to eleven.

As the tablets stopped fizzing, she drank the concoction. 'Well,' she observed, 'that's all the breakfast I'm having.' And she turned around smartly, intending to go back upstairs again, when suddenly she noticed, sitting in a corner, Claudio's brown leather holdall, from the look of it fully packed.

She paused, straggling to ignore the way her heart had shrunk in pain and flicked what she hoped was a mildly curious glance in his direction.

'Are you leaving?' she wanted to know.

'I don't think there's much point in my staying on any longer.' Claudio took a bite of his brioche and washed it down with *caffelatte*. 'I've decided to get out of your hair and go back home.'

Rachel knew that should please her, and she tried to look as though it did. She smiled. 'That's good. I'm sure we'll both be happier.' But as she looked at him her heart was filling with misery. She was crazy, but she didn't want him to leave.

She stared at the floor, silently wishing she could tell him, that she could just fall into his arms and confess how she felt.

And that was when she experienced her first flash of memory. Suddenly, vividly, she was starting to recall last night. She was recalling how he had scooped her up into his arms and carried her upstairs to her room. And, worse, she was recalling how, quite wantonly, she'd kissed him.

'As soon as your mother and Dino arrive, ask them to come to my place.' Quite oblivious of the anguish seething within her, Claudio was polishing off the remains of his brioche and telling her, 'I think it's probably better if we have our confrontation at my place. And there's really no need for you to be there.'

Rachel looked at him in blank incomprehension for a moment. She'd totally forgotten about his quarrel with Dino and her mother. Then she nodded distractedly. 'If that's what you want. When they come, I'll tell them you're waiting for them at your place.'

'And don't say anything about us for the moment. If they discover it was all a trick, they might decide to do another bunk, and it would be a shame to waste all that effort we've put in.' Claudio smiled an amused smile as he wiped his mouth with his napkin. 'I'll tell them when I've finished discussing business. And, of course, once they get back here you can tell them yourself.'

Rachel nodded a little absently. 'OK,' she agreed. 'That's what I'll do if you think that's best.' But she was only half concentrating on what she was saying, for suddenly she was remembering something else about last night. She was remembering how she'd put her arms around him and slipped her hand inside his shirt. Good grief, she was thinking, I really was drunk!

Claudio dropped his napkin back on the table-top and reached into the breast pocket of the white shirt he was wearing. He drew out a folded cheque and tossed it down in front of him.

'This is payment for what I've consumed while I've been here,' he explained. 'I think you'll find it more than covers the few drinks and the couple of coffees I've had.'

Rachel nodded without bothering to glance at the cheque. If he said it was sufficient, then she had no doubt it was. Besides, it was hard to give much attention to such matters when all at once her memory was running riot. For suddenly she could recall not only the kiss, not only the hand slipped inside his shirt, but also how she'd invited him to undress her and even brazenly suggested that he join her in bed.

I'm going to be sick, she thought. What must he think of me? He must think I'm a total, shameless tramp.

Claudio had picked up his cup of *caffelatte* and was draining it quickly. Then he was glancing at his watch and rising to his feet. 'I think I ought to go. I've got some phone calls to make. I'll leave you in peace to nurse your hangover.'

But as he bent to pick up his leather holdall Rachel cleared her throat and spoke. 'I've a feeling,' she said in a small, nervous voice, 'that I made a terrible fool of myself last night.' Her hands were clenched into fists as she spoke.

Claudio paused and turned to look at her. 'I don't remember that,' he said.

Rachel could feel her stomach as heavy as lead inside her. She clenched her fists tighter and said again, since he obviously hadn't understood her, 'Last night... You must have got a terrible impression...' She pulled a face of shameful misery. 'You have no idea how awful I feel.'

Claudio was still watching her and though there was a light smile on his lips his eyes held a look of gentle understanding. 'Don't feel awful,' he told her. 'There's nothing to feel awful about. Besides——' he reached out and touched her chin with his fingertips '—to tell the truth, I really can't remember a thing.'

Rachel felt a rush of pure love for him. This was the last thing she had expected—that he would show such kindness, that he would try to save her face. He's wonderful, she thought. The kindest man I've ever known. It's little wonder that I love him.

But these thoughts were scary. She shouldn't be thinking them. He might be acting kindly, but he still didn't love her. And if she showed how she felt for him she would only end up looking a fool again.

And that was why she said, 'I don't know how it happened. The wine... You know... I drank too much... I hadn't a clue what I was doing.'

'Sure. I know that.' His fingertips still brushed her. 'I could see you definitely were not in full control.'

'I was out of my head.'

The touch of him was thrilling. She longed to lower her head and brush her lips against his fingers. And, worse, she longed to fall into his arms and kiss him.

She felt a sudden dart of pain and panic within her. It was the slippery slope. She would end up crashing again. And she mustn't. She couldn't let herself. It would be unforgivable.

Looking into his face, she grabbed at the first lie that occurred to her. 'I was all mixed up. I thought it was Mark I was with, not you.' She forced a lame laugh. 'It's terrible what alcohol can do.'

'It certainly is.' His hand dropped away. He took a step back. 'But don't worry about it.' Then he bent down quickly to pick up his holdall. 'I'd better be off now. Remember what I told you. Send Dino and your mother to my place as soon as they get here.'

Then he was heading across the kitchen, pausing only to add, 'I'll see you around. Enjoy the rest of your holiday.'

A moment later, he was heading out through the kitchen door. Rachel watched him go, trying to take in what had just happened. He's gone, she thought numbly. Just like that, it's over.

Feeling suddenly cold, she stared at the kitchen door. I'll never see him again. It's over. It's over. A sob broke in her throat. She felt a vast plummet of despair. He's gone from my life. Gone forever.

CHAPTER EIGHT

RACHEL'S mother and Dino arrived back just after three.

Rachel was sitting on the veranda staring blankly at a magazine which she had long ago given up trying to read. And through her misery she was actually quite pleased to see them as their little Lancia came screeching to a halt at the end of the driveway.

'I hope you didn't drive like that all the way from Capri.' As her mother leapt from the passenger seat and came rushing towards her, Rachel smiled at her wryly and bent to kiss her on both cheeks. 'I promise you the situation really doesn't warrant it.'

'If half of what I've heard is true, it most certainly does warrant it!' Her mother was in no mood for jocularity. She glanced past Rachel, scowling with disapproval. 'Where is Claudio? Is he here?'

'No, he's not. He's at home.'

Rachel paused to glance at Dino, who was greeting her with a, 'Hello, Rachel,' as he came to join them.

'Hi, Dino,' she responded. Then, addressing both of them, she continued, 'he told me to ask you to go to his place immediately. Apparently, there's something he needs to discuss.'

At that, Rachel couldn't help but notice the look that passed between them. It was a worried look, and on Dino's side even a little guilty, she thought.

Then her mother turned back to Rachel. 'But what about you and Claudio? I've really been hearing the most scandalous stories.'

Rachel had to suppress a blush, along with a stab of sheer misery. 'Then I'm afraid your informants have been exaggerating,' she told her mother. 'I assure you nothing even remotely scandalous has been going on.'

Then, before her mother could interrupt, she insisted in a firm voice, 'Go and see Claudio first and we'll talk about it later.' She forced what she hoped was a reassuring smile, for she could see that her mother was genuinely concerned. 'Go on,' she urged. 'And stop worrying about nothing.'

Half an hour later, after a quick shower and a change of clothes, her mother and Dino were setting off down the drive again.

Left alone, Rachel did her best to relax. She went for a swim in the pool, then stretched out on one of the sunbeds, but it was hopeless; her mind was going round in circles. She kept wondering what was going on right now with her mother and Dino. But, most of all, she simply kept thinking of Claudio.

Every time she closed her eyes, his face appeared before her—that wonderful face with its dark eyes and easy smile that could turn her blood to powder and fill her soul with light. And all the time she kept thinking, I'm never going to see him again. And it tore her to pieces. It was too cruel to bear.

I wish I'd never come. If I'd never come, I'd never have met him. And if I'd never met him, I'd never have fallen in love with him and I wouldn't be feeling the way I do.

And yet, in her heart, though the pain was fierce and terrible, Rachel knew she wouldn't have traded for all the tranquillity in the world the magical few days they'd had together. Those were beyond price and she would treasure the memory of them always.

At least I know what love is now, she told herself bravely. And surely next time when I fall in love I'll be a little luckier? Surely next time it'll be with someone who's able to return my love?

But somehow that plea seemed to offer little hope. It was quite impossible to imagine ever falling in love with anyone else.

It was nearly two and a half hours later when Dino and her mother got back. Rachel, still in her swimsuit, was sitting on the kitchen patio, daydreaming over a glass of iced tea. And, since the daydreams were all hopeless daydreams of Claudio, she was rather grateful for the interruption when the two of them appeared.

As her mother came and plonked herself down at the table beside her, there was a look of unmistakable relief on her face.

'Well,' she said, 'that was quite a marathon, but at least we've finally got everything sorted out.' She shook her head at Rachel. 'Including these stories abut you. Claudio tells us they're all gross exaggerations and that you and he are just friends, nothing more.' She fixed Rachel with a look, waiting for confirmation.

So that was what he'd said? That the two of them were just friends? Rachel had to grit her teeth against the pain of rejection that swept through her.

She took a mouthful of iced tea and told her mother, 'Isn't that what I told you? That what you'd heard was an exaggeration? There's nothing going on between Claudio and me.'

Quite clearly, she reflected, he'd said nothing about it being a trick. And, come to think of it, that was probably for the best. It made it easier for her mother and Dino to swallow, and it saved any unnecessary aggravation between them and herself.

But she was keen to change the subject. 'So,' she asked her mother, 'how did the rest of your business go?'

For the next hour or so her mother and Dino proceeded to tell her, pouring out their hearts to her in their relief. And as Rachel listened it was all a total revelation.

One of the first things she discovered was that what Claudio had told her about the house was true. It was still legally his, though he was selling it to Dino. And, just as he'd claimed, Dino had fallen down on the payments—on top of owing him a quite separate and substantial sum of money.

She also discovered that her mother had known nothing about any of this—at least, not until last night, when she had winkled the truth out of Dino.

'I was stupid.' Dino cast a contrite look at his wife. 'I allowed things to get totally out of control. In the end, I owed Claudio so much money I just couldn't see any way of repaying him. Then when he started insisting I got angry and made matters worse.'

He shook his grey head and explained to Rachel, 'You see, I was terrified we'd end up on the street, and I couldn't allow that to happen to your mother.'

Emily patted Dino's hand then turned to her daughter. 'It was all because of me that he did it. He knew I'd had a hard life before I met him and he was determined to try and make it up to me. That was why he borrowed from Claudio—though he pretended it was for his business—so he could buy me diamonds and take me on fancy holidays.' She frowned. 'He didn't realise all I wanted was him.'

Rachel was feeling distinctly moved by these surprise revelations. Dino had acted foolishly, but he must love her mother very much, just as her mother quite clearly loved him.

'So is that why,' she asked, 'you took off to Capri? To try to get away from Claudio?'

Dino answered first. 'I made some excuse to your mother. I told her it was very important that we go there...' He dropped his eyes. 'But yes, you're right, that's why I did it. I just couldn't cope with the pressure any more. And I thought if we just disappeared maybe he'd leave us alone——'

Emily cut in, 'I hated going off and leaving you, but I knew something was wrong and I had to stand by Dino, even though he refused to tell me what was going on.' She glanced with gentle reproof at her husband. 'But then after he made me phone you about getting the files to our solicitor... well, that was when

I started insisting he tell me. And bit by bit the whole story came out.'

Dino looked relieved even just thinking about it. 'I wish now I'd confessed sooner. Emily helped me to get it all straight in my mind—and she also insisted that we come back and face the music...'

Rachel had to smile wryly at that. 'So you were planning to come back anyway—even if Claudio and I——?' She stopped herself and rephrased that. 'Even if you hadn't heard all those stories about us?' As her mother nodded, she added, 'So what happened when you went to see him?'

Emily sat back in her seat and pulled a face of disbelief. 'Well, that was by far the biggest surprise of all! He was so nice about it. As soon as Dino apologised and said he wanted to make amends, he simply couldn't have been more decent.

'So we've come to an arrangement. We'll pay back our debts gradually and in the meantime we get to keep the house.'

Rachel was glad for them and really not surprised in the least that Claudio in the end had acted so generously. He's a good man, she thought wistfully. How else could I love him?

To her mother she said, 'I'm glad you got it sorted out.'

But her mother was still pondering this new side she'd seen to Claudio. 'You know,' she mused, 'I think maybe I've been wrong about him. He's not such a bully after all. As soon as we started being straight with him, he really couldn't have been more kind.'

Dino hung his head. 'It was my fault you thought he was a bully. But he's never been a bully. He's nobody's fool, but he's not a bully. I'd no business ever saying he was.'

All this sudden praise of Claudio was having a disastrous effect on Rachel. All at once, her breath seemed to be catching in her throat, her heart was racing again and her palms felt quite damp.

She had to get away. She started to stand up. 'I'm going upstairs to change.' She forced a brittle smile. 'When I come back, you can tell me all about Capri.'

But her mother was continuing her musings about Claudio. 'You know, this afternoon I really rather liked him.' Then she frowned. 'It's just a pity he treats women so disgracefully.'

Rachel could not let that pass. 'He doesn't treat women disgracefully.' Not even, she added silently, remembering last night, when they virtually demand to be treated disgracefully. 'He can be a bit wild at times, but he treats women with respect. At least,' she added firmly, 'that's been my experience.'

Her mother was staring at her open-mouthed. 'I'm very glad to hear it.'

But, before she could say another word, Rachel was turning away and striding back into the kitchen, her heart a tumult of all sorts of emotions—pain and pride and love and anguish. Though just for a moment the greatest of these was pride—pride in Claudio for being the most wonderful man alive and pride a little also in herself for having chosen such a man to fall in love with.

* * *

But the most wonderful man alive still didn't love her. In fact, it was quite clear that she never crossed his mind.

A week passed and Rachel heard nothing from him. Not that she'd expected to, but she'd hoped none the less. And now, she was telling herself, it was time to stop hoping. It was time to go home. To put some distance between them. Time she started getting him out of her head.

For as long as she stayed here she knew that would be impossible. Every time she visited Florence she was constantly looking out for him, hoping he might appear round some street corner. At the villa, every time the phone rang she prayed it might be him. And it was starting to hurt too much. She must be brave and make the break.

So at dinner one evening she told her mother and Dino, 'I've decided to go back a little earlier than planned.' Then, as they started to protest, she added decisively, 'I've managed to get booked on a flight the day after tomorrow.'

It was a *fait accompli*. There was no way she could backtrack. And it was too late now for anyone to try and talk her out of it.

She sighed with relief. She had less than two days of purgatory to go. Somehow she would manage to live through that.

For her last day Rachel had planned a special programme for herself.

She would spend the day in Florence doing all the things she hadn't done yet—like visiting the

Accademia and the Bargello, and maybe even managing to fit in the purchase of a pair of shoes—then in the evening she would treat her mother and Dino to dinner. The day would go like a flash, which was precisely what she wanted. And before she had time to blink she'd be on the plane back to England.

She spent the morning in the Bargello admiring the priceless sculptures there, then she found a trattoria in the city centre and took her time enjoying the *menu turistico*. She had decided, as a special treat, to keep the Accademia till last, for that was where Michelangelo's original David was housed. It would provide a fitting climax to her sightseeing, she'd decided. Nothing, after all, could possibly top that!

And the experience was even more amazing than she'd expected.

She made her way along the gallery lined with the powerful prisoner statues to where, in its simple glass-domed rotunda, the breathtaking marble David stood. Then she just stood there in awe and looked up at it in silence. It was the most wonderful, most beautiful thing she had ever seen.

For a long time she just stood there, like the other tourists, in admiring silence, smiling to herself, feeling happily uplifted, temporarily forgetting the pain in her heart.

Then, satisfied at last, she turned away to leave and began to make her way back along the gallery, her mind still filled with the powerful beauty of the David. But she stopped in her tracks. Surely she must be dreaming? Suddenly her heart had stopped in her chest.

But she wasn't dreaming. He had been standing by the row of prisoners, a tall, athletic figure in beige trousers and a white-striped shirt, his jacket slung lightly over one shoulder.

And now, silently, he was stepping towards her.

'Rachel,' he said softly.

Rachel looked back at him, feeling as though she was dying on the spot, the emotions that suddenly filled her almost too violent to cope with. She felt helpless, stunned, totally vulnerable—and filled with a sudden fierce rush of sheer joy that wrapped around her poor splintered heart like warm honey.

'Claudio!' she breathed. 'What are you doing here?'

By way of a response Claudio stepped forward and took her hand. 'I want to talk,' he told her. Then, before she could protest, he was leading her along the gallery to the exit. A moment later they were outside in the warm afternoon sunshine.

'What is this all about?' Rachel tried a token protest, half-heartedly pulling away from him as he began to propel her along the street. 'You can't just suddenly appear and kidnap me like this!'

Claudio paused and turned to look at her and for the first time Rachel noticed the tense, slightly strained look he had about the eyes. As she peered at him, confused and curious, and now suddenly also a little concerned, he took her hand in both of his and held it tightly for a moment.

'I'm not kidnapping you. But we have to talk. And we have to talk now. I just spoke to your mother on the phone half an hour ago. She told me you're all set to leave tomorrow.'

Rachel nodded.

'Then it has to be now.' He smiled grimly. 'Let's go to my place. We'll be private there.'

The silver Maserati was parked at the end of the street. Rachel climbed in and sat nervously staring at the hem of her skirt. And her gaze never shifted throughout the twenty-minute journey up into the sweet-scented hills of Fiesole.

In fact, no part of her moved. She felt oddly frozen. And not a word passed between them, though the air was electric. But this was not a time for small talk or trivialities, Rachel sensed. Quite clearly, he had something very important to say to her. And as they sped up the winding road she tried not to guess what it might be. It couldn't be what she was hoping, though she wasn't even sure what she was hoping. The truth was she was far too scared to hope. Fear was what filled her. Fear that all that awaited her was more hurt and rejection and bitter disappointment.

And now they were passing through a high arched gateway, impressively flanked by a pair of stone eagles, then heading up a wide driveway, between columns of green cypresses, to come to halt outside a magnificent villa.

So, this is where he lives, Rachel thought to herself dully, gazing up at the beautiful house with its rosy stone walls, its flower-bedecked balconies and red-tiled turrets. She had often wondered what his home was like and now she knew. It was like something out of a fairy-tale, she thought. A little like him.

But she wasn't a part of that fairy-tale. She felt dread touch her heart as he said to her now, 'Here we are. Let's go in.'

As he began to climb from the car, Rachel pressed back in her seat. And for the first time since climbing into the car she actually dared to look at him. 'What's this all about? I'm not sure it's a good idea. Maybe it would be better if you just took me back into town.'

'I'm going to do no such thing. You're not escaping me now.' Claudio climbed out, slammed the door, then came round to her side and proceeded to pull open the passenger door. Then he was holding out his hand to her. 'Don't worry, I won't eat you.'

That was not what she was afraid of. She wouldn't have minded being eaten. But she did not say so. In fact, she said nothing. Instead, a little stiffly, she found herself smiling back at him, responding to the wry smile that had accompanied the remark. It was hopeless, but she could never resist him when he smiled.

They made their way in silence through the big front door and across an airy, marble-tiled hallway. 'Let's go through to the *salotto*,' Claudio suggested. Then he was leading her into an elegant, spacious drawing-room whose polished parquet floor was strewn with soft-coloured rugs and where magnificent Etruscan lamps stood on low, carved tables. It was the most beautiful room Rachel had ever set eyes on.

'Take a seat.' Claudio waved her towards one of the cream-coloured sofas arranged beneath a huge, gilt-framed mirror. 'Tell me. What would you like to drink?'

Rachel hesitated for just a second. Then, 'Mineral water,' she said firmly. She'd been on the point of requesting a large vodka and tonic, something with a bit of steel in it to settle her nerves, but just in time she'd recalled her last encounter with the demon alcohol. She had no desire to land him with a reprise of that!

As Claudio smiled, Rachel could see that he'd read her thoughts perfectly. But he made no comment and did not try to change her mind. 'OK,' he said. 'Personally, I'm going to have something stronger.' Then he crossed to the bar in the corner and poured himself a stiff whisky.

He came back, handed her mineral water with a slice of lemon and some ice, took a mouthful of his Scotch and seated himself on the sofa opposite her. Then he fixed her with a look and came straight to the point.

'So, you were planning on leaving without even telling me? Don't you think you might at least have rung me up to say goodbye?'

Rachel felt a plummet inside her. Was that why he'd dragged her here? To chastise her? To insist on a formal farewell?

She took a deep, calming breath, for her heart was suddenly racing. 'I can't see how it matters to you whether I say goodbye or not.'

'Can't you?' One eyebrow lifted.

'No, I can't, as a matter of fact. I'm sure you have much more pressing matters on your mind.' She took a mouthful of her mineral water, her fingers tight around the glass, and stared down at the sliver of lemon for a moment. I was right, I should never have come here, she was thinking.

There was a silence for a moment, then Claudio spoke again.

'I suppose these "much more pressing matters" you have in mind are matters of the female variety?' he said softly. As Rachel glanced up at him, taken by surprise, he continued, still in that soft tone, 'Well, I can hardly blame you. You have every reason to believe that.'

'Yes, I do.'

Her heart was jumping, her fingers like claws around her glass. She wanted to lay it down, but she was afraid she might spill it. Why is he doing this? Why is he torturing me? Her brain was reeling. Doesn't he know I don't want to talk about his girlfriends?

But he was continuing, 'It's my own fault. I made you believe it.' Then he leaned forward and frowned at her. 'But really it's all a total fabrication.'

'Hah! That's a likely story!' Rachel sat back in her seat defensively. What did he take her for? He had to be joking!

But there was no sign of humour in his eyes. In fact, they looked slightly haunted as he sat there, very still, and watched her for a moment.

'Do you really believe all those stories your mother told you,' he asked at last, 'about my being some kind of sex maniac?'

'No.' She had long ago ceased to believe that. 'I accept that was a bit of an exaggeration. But all the same——' she narrowed sceptical dark hazel eyes at him '—I've seen for myself that your love life keeps you pretty busy. Not,' she added hastily, 'that that's any concern of mine. You're a free man, after all. You can do what you like.'

'Yes, I can—and what I'd like to do right now is convince you that appearances can sometimes be deceiving. Or, let me put it another way...' Claudio paused for a moment and laid his whisky glass down on a nearby table. 'The truth is, Rachel, I've been playing a game with you. Trying to give you the impression that I have a whole string of girlfriends.' He smiled a contrite smile. 'Perhaps I succeeded too well.'

Rachel was frowning in bafflement. 'I don't believe you. After all, I've witnessed the evidence with my own eyes. And anyway, why would you want to do a thing like that?'

'To make you jealous.'

'To make me jealous?' Her heart jolted inside her. All at once, she could feel a nervous fluttering in her throat. She sat very still, hardly daring to look at him, and laughed a nervous, brittle laugh. 'That's ridiculous! What about that girl I saw you with at your studio?'

'Lisa? she's an ex-girlfriend, now a client. I'm designing a house for her and her fiancé.'

That was a good one! Rachel laughed disbelievingly, recalling the arm around Lisa's slim waist. She made a face at Claudio. 'She didn't look very ex to me.'

Claudio smiled a narrow smile. 'I heard the lift coming. I knew it was you, so I put on a show.'

That fluttering pulse in her throat was growing stronger. Rachel had to concentrate very hard on her breathing.

'And what about that date you had the other night? Are you trying to tell me that was a set-up as well?'

'A total set-up. I went to dinner with some friends. *Male* friends,' he emphasised. 'Then we sat up playing cards until late.'

'And the other night...? What about Kirsten? That wasn't a set-up!'

Claudio shook his head. 'I didn't see Kirsten,' he said.

'But what about that phone call? What about that?' suddenly, in a painful flood, it was all coming back to her. Then, hating the way she was cross-questioning him like this—she sounded like some insecure, possessive girlfriend!—Rachel flared across at him with sudden impatience, 'Why are you telling me this ridiculous fairy-story? It doesn't matter to me how many girlfriends you've got!'

'Doesn't it?' Something retreated at the back of his eyes. He sat back and watched her in silence for a moment. 'So, my campaign to make you jealous failed, after all?' he said at last.

Rachel swallowed hard. Her brain was swimming and that pulse in her throat was driving her crazy. She said, carefully avoiding answering his question. 'Why on earth would you want to make me jealous?'

'Perhaps because *I* was jealous. A kind of tit for tat. Or perhaps in an effort to try and draw things to a head.' He sighed. 'I was trying to replace Mark in your heart.'

Rachel had to lay her glass down now. Holding it was too much of an effort. Every muscle in her body seemed to have turned to paper. She opened her mouth to speak, but then shut it again, helplessly, suddenly not trusting herself to sound coherent. Her brain was spinning like a top.

And now, to make matters worse, Claudio was rising to his feet and coming across to seat himself alongside her. He sat without touching her, though his nearness engulfed her, and said in a tone whose intensity was almost scary, 'Mark's not the man for you. It would be a mistake for you to marry him. I can feel it in my bones. I've always felt it.'

'Claudio...' Rachel hesitated, transfixed by the black eyes. The emotion she could see in them was eating her alive. Never before had she seen such fierce emotion in a pair of eyes.

'I know you've already agreed to marry him...' His voice broke slightly as he continued, 'And maybe it isn't my place to interfere... But you'd be making a mistake and I can't let you do that. Rachel, I——'

'I haven't agreed to marry him.' Rachel spoke quickly. Her mouth felt dry. She was still trying to catch her breath. 'He asked me just before I came here, but I turned him down.' She glanced down into her lap. 'I knew it wouldn't be right. It was all over between me and Mark before I even came here.'

'But I thought——'

'I misled you.' She wondered if she dared look up again. Her eyes were fixed blindly on the hem of her skirt. 'I did it——' She paused. 'I did it because of you.' Then, taking hold of her courage, she looked up at him quickly, suddenly feeling hugely, helplessly vulnerable, but knowing she had to see the reaction in his eyes. She smiled a stiff smile. 'A kind of tit for tat.'

Disbelief filled his eyes. Wonderfully happy disbelief. And suddenly, in an instant, that haunted look had fled.

'Tit for tat?' He laughed. 'You really mean that? You mean you were playing the same game as me?'

'It looks like it.' As she looked at him, Rachel was feeling quite giddy. Am I dreaming? she was asking herself. Is any of this real?

But the next moment, beyond a doubt, she knew it was real. For, before she could catch her breath, Claudio was reaching out towards her and gathering her with gentle desperation into his arms. Then his lips were crushing hers and her heart was soaring in her chest as he whispered against her hair, 'I love you, Rachel.'

'And I love you!' She kissed him back with passion. Her soaring heart was bursting with happiness inside her.

For a long, long time he held her close to him, kissing her hair, her face, her throat. Then he drew back to look at her. 'I'm the man for you, you know. I'm the man you should marry. I hope you realise that. And if you don't I intend to use all my powers to persuade you.'

Rachel looked back at him, a little stunned by the speed at which all of this was happening. 'And how,' she asked lightly, 'do you intend to persuade me?'

'A thousand ways.' He caressed her cheek with his fingers. 'I'll send you flowers, I'll buy you presents, I'll take you to visit wonderful places...' Then he paused and seemed to hold his breath for a moment. 'But most of all I'll show you how much I love you every single time I make love to you,' he told her.

Rachel's mouth had gone quite dry again. That 'every single time' had caused a fierce, hungry tightening in the pit of her stomach.

'Really?' she said, swallowing hard.

'Perhaps I should show you what I mean?' Claudio kissed her lips softly, with one hand caressing her breast as he spoke. Then as she shuddered and closed her eyes suddenly he was rising to his feet, at the same time gathering her unresisting body from the sofa. 'I suggest we go upstairs,' he said.

Rachel could only nod in response, twining her arms round his neck as he carried her across the *salotto* and out into the hall. And as she leaned her face against his shoulder and kissed his cheek gently she was remembering that other time at her mother's villa when they had enacted a scene very similar to this.

Only this time she was perfectly sober. She knew what she was doing. And she would remember every single detail of what was about to happen. She felt quite breathless at the thought. What was about to happen would be wonderful. Hadn't she always known that Claudio would be a wonderful lover?

And he was. He was the lover every woman had ever dreamed of—sensitive, exciting, tireless, masterful—as he unhurriedly proceeded to demonstrate.

He laid her on the bed and covered her with kisses, caressing her with his hands and with his lips and with his body, drawing her into an ever-tightening spiral of excitement as item by item he peeled away her clothes.

And suddenly they were lying naked together, their warmth mingling, their bodies entwining, his hardness and her softness striking sparks off each other, both gasping at the sheer strength of the yearning that filled them.

Rachel felt slack with desire as his hands caressed her, his fingers exploring every shivering dip and curve.

'*Amore*,' he murmured as he sat astride her, his palms cupping her breasts, his thumbs strumming the hard peaks.

Then, making her shudder, he was lowering himself on top of her to take each rosy nipple in turn into his mouth, his tongue driving her crazy, sending a fire raging through her. Suddenly the longing in her was too powerful to bear.

'Oh, Claudio!' she breathed. 'I love you! I love you!' She had never believed it possible to want a man so much.

He had understood the need in her. He raised his head to look at her, his eyes pouring into her as he stroked the hair from her face.

'Now,' he told her, 'I am going to make you mine.'

Rachel felt a wave of love surge through her, so fierce, so powerful, she felt like weeping. And suddenly she had to tell him.

She looked into his eyes. 'You're the first, you know.'

'The first?' He paused. 'You really mean that, *amore*?'

Rachel nodded, feeling touched by the hesitation in his eyes. And suddenly she knew there was something else she had to tell him.

'I don't need flowers or presents or trips to wonderful places to persuade me. I already know you're the man for me.' She reached up and kissed the lips she adored. 'There could never be any other. The only man for me is you.'

'Does that mean you'll marry me?'

Rachel nodded. 'Yes, it does.'

Claudio smiled, then he closed his eyes. '*Amore!*' he whispered. Then he bent down to kiss her with all the passion that seethed within him. 'You're going nowhere tomorrow, you know that?' he growled at her. 'Except maybe down to San Cappano to break the news to your mother. I shall never let you leave my side again,' he vowed.

'I shall never want to leave it.' Rachel trembled as she kissed him. 'Never, never!' she breathed.

And as she gazed at him, glorying in the wonderful sight of him and the wonderful love she could see shining in his eyes, she knew that, finally, the happiness she had dreamed of was hers.

She flung her arms around his neck. 'Oh, Claudio, I love you!'

And a moment later she let out a cry of exquisite pleasure as their two bodies slipped together and at last became one.

Harlequin Romance ®

New from Harlequin Romance a very special six-book series by

MIDNIGHT SONS

DEBBIE MACOMBER

The town of Hard Luck, Alaska, needs women!

The O'Halloran brothers, who run a bush-plane service called **Midnight Sons**, are heading a campaign to attract women to Hard Luck. (*Location: north of the Arctic Circle. Population: 150—mostly men!*)

"Debbie Macomber's *Midnight Sons* series is a delightful romantic saga. And each book is a powerful, engaging story in its own right. Unforgettable!"

—Linda Lael Miller

TITLE IN THE MIDNIGHT SONS SERIES:

BRIDE'S BAY RESORT

UNLOCK THE DOOR TO GREAT ROMANCE AT BRIDE'S BAY RESORT

Join Harlequin's new across-the-lines series, set in an exclusive hotel on an island off the coast of South Carolina.

Seven of your favorite authors will bring you exciting stories about fascinating heroes and heroines discovering love at Bride's Bay Resort.

Look for these fabulous stories coming to a store near you beginning in January 1996.

Harlequin American Romance #613 in January
Matchmaking Baby by Cathy Gillen Thacker

Harlequin Presents #1794 in February
Indiscretions by Robyn Donald

Harlequin Intrigue #362 in March
Love and Lies by Dawn Stewardson

Harlequin Romance #3404 in April
Make Believe Engagement by Day Leclaire

Harlequin Temptation #588 in May
Stranger in the Night by Roseanne Williams

Harlequin Superromance #695 in June
Married to a Stranger by Connie Bennett

Harlequin Historicals #324 in July
Dulcie's Gift by Ruth Langan

Visit Bride's Bay Resort each month wherever Harlequin books are sold.

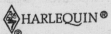

HARLEQUIN ®

BBAYG

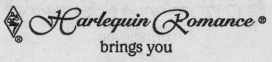

Harlequin Romance ®

brings you

How the West was Wooed!

We've rounded up twelve of our most popular authors, and the result is a whole year of romance, Western style. Every month we'll be bringing you a spirited, independent woman whose heart is about to be lassoed by a rugged, handsome, one-hundred-percent cowboy! Watch for...

- March: **CLANTON'S WOMAN**—Patricia Knoll

- April: **A DANGEROUS MAGIC**—Patricia Wilson

- May: **THE BADLANDS BRIDE**—Rebecca Winters

- June: **RUNAWAY WEDDING**—Ruth Jean Dale

- July: **A RANCH, A RING AND EVERYTHING**—Val Daniels

HITCH-2

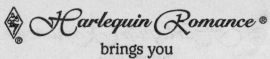

Harlequin Romance ®

brings you

HOLDING OUT FOR A HERO ★

Some men are worth waiting for!

They're handsome, they're charming but, best of all,
they're single! Twelve lucky women are about to
discover that finding Mr. Right is not a problem—it's
holding on to him.

In March the series continues with

#3401 THE ONLY MAN FOR MAGGIE
by Leigh Michaels

Karr Elliot wanted Maggie off his property but not out
of his life. But Maggie didn't want a man—she wanted
her own apartment!

Hold out for Harlequin Romance's heroes in
coming months...

- April: **THE RIGHT KIND OF MAN**—Jessica Hart

- May: **MOVING IN WITH ADAM**—Jeanne Allan

- June: **THE PARENT TRAP**—Leigh Michaels